GIRLS' Weekend in VEGAS

Four friends, four dream weddings!

On a girly weekend in Las Vegas, best friends
Alex, Molly, Serena and Jayne are supposed to
just have fun and forget men—but they end up
meeting their perfect matches! Will the love
they find in Vegas stay in Vegas?

Find out in this sassy, fun and wildly romantic
miniseries all about love and friendship!

This month meet Jayne in

Wedding Date with the Best Man by Melissa McClone

Dear Reader,

Las Vegas has always been one of my favorite escapes. When I lived in Phoenix, Arizona, and could take advantage of cheap shuttle flights, my girlfriends and I spent many weekends lounging by hotel pools, scrounging out inexpensive buffets, window-shopping and exploring casinos.

When I moved to San Francisco I continued to meet my friends for weekend getaways to Las Vegas. We all cherished the opportunity to dish about men and careers, recover from broken hearts, relax at a show or bond over blackjack.

The year I turned twenty-six, eleven friends—male and female—joined me for an amazing birthday celebration weekend. I've always been a fan of castles, so we stayed at the Excalibur Hotel on the Las Vegas strip. My birthday dinner was a banquet show, complete with gorgeous jousting knights. A photo from that night—the silly grins, the extravagant medieval costumes—sits in my study today. It was a weekend to remember. Good times with great friends.

Those memories played a part in my writing *Wedding Date with the Best Man*. When your heart is broken, like Jayne Cavendish's, nothing beats a weekend away with your closest girlfriends.

Jayne is happy when her three best friends unexpectedly find love in Sin City. But it isn't until she returns on a visit with sexy Tristan MacGregor that she discovers Las Vegas can be as romantic as Paris.

Enjoy!

Melissa

MELISSA MCCLONE
Wedding Date with the Best Man

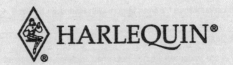

TORONTO • NEW YORK • LONDON
AMSTERDAM • PARIS • SYDNEY • HAMBURG
STOCKHOLM • ATHENS • TOKYO • MILAN • MADRID
PRAGUE • WARSAW • BUDAPEST • AUCKLAND

Recycling programs
for this product may
not exist in your area.

ISBN-13: 978-0-373-17683-0

WEDDING DATE WITH THE BEST MAN

First North American Publication 2010.

With a degree in mechanical engineering from Stanford University, the last thing **Melissa McClone** ever thought she would be doing was writing romance novels. But analyzing engines for a major U.S. airline just couldn't compete with her happily-ever-afters. When she isn't writing, caring for her three young children or doing laundry, Melissa loves to curl up on the couch with a cup of tea, her cats and a good book. She enjoys watching home decorating shows to get ideas for her house—a 1939 cottage that is *slowly* being renovated. Melissa lives in Lake Oswego, Oregon, with her own real-life-hero husband, two daughters, a son, two lovable but oh-so-spoiled indoor cats and a no-longer-stray outdoor kitty that decided to call the garage home. Melissa loves to hear from her readers. You can write to her at P.O. Box 63, Lake Oswego, OR 97034, U.S.A., or contact her via her Web site, www.melissamcclone.com.

To Virginia Kantra for her
wonderful writing insights, support and friendship.

Special thanks to Amy Danicic, Terri Reed
and Girls' Weekend in Vegas authors
Myrna Mackenzie, Shirley Jump and Jackie Braun,
and editor Meg Lewis.

CHAPTER ONE

CONVERSATION and laughter surrounded Jayne Cavendish. Sitting at a small table tucked away in a corner of the Victorian Tea House, she glanced around the room.

Pairs of women sat at tables nestled among potted plants and curio cabinets filled with an eclectic collection of teacups and saucers. Everyone seemed to be having a great time at one of San Diego's favorite Old Town establishments. Everyone but her.

She stared at her steaming cup of Earl Gray, wishing she could conjure up one of her three best friends. She missed Alex, Molly and Serena so much.

Sure, they kept in touch via phone calls, texting and Facebook. Twitter came in handy, too. Alex jetted back from Las Vegas when she could, and Molly would be returning once her and Linc's dream house was built and his business moved here, but it wasn't the same as all four of them living in San Diego, dishing face-to-face, getting pedicures and going to tea.

Jayne sank in her chair, feeling as buoyant as a deflated hot air balloon.

Maybe coming to the teahouse this Saturday afternoon hadn't been such a good idea. She remembered her first visit, when her then-fiancé's sisters had thrown Jayne a bridal shower. That 'welcome to the family' party seemed like years ago, even though it had been only months.

So much had changed since then. She touched the bare ring finger on her left hand. So much still hadn't changed.

At least not for her.

Jayne looked down at the silver-rimmed plate containing two golden-brown scones and a dollop of honey butter.

Too bad she wasn't hungry.

Uh-oh. If she weren't careful she'd soon be hosting a pity party for herself. Jayne sipped her tea to clear her head.

No sense wallowing in the past.

Her teacup clinked against the saucer as she placed it on the table.

So what if memories of her bridal shower with the Strickland sisters were bittersweet? Jayne had other memories, good memories, of subsequent visits here with Alex, Molly and Serena. Her three friends might not be related to Jayne by blood, but she considered them the sisters of her heart. Nothing, not distance or their marriages, would ever change that.

Determined to make peace with the present and enjoy herself, Jayne removed a library book—the latest offering from a top personal finance guru—from her purse. She opened it to her bookmark: a picturesque postcard with a palm tree arcing over a crescent of sugar-white sand and turquoise water stretching all the way to the horizon.

A perfect place for a honeymoon, she thought with a twinge of regret.

No regrets.

She straightened.

So what if things hadn't turned out with Rich Strickland as she'd planned? Because of what had happened—er, hadn't happened—her three best friends had found the loves of their lives. Jayne could never regret the end of her engagement and the wild weekend with her friends in Las Vegas afterward that had brought romance and so much happiness to the three people who mattered most in her life.

She flipped over the postcard she'd received two months ago and reread Serena's loopy, almost whimsical handwriting.

Jayne
Having a great time! This trip was the perfect way to celebrate Jonas' election victory and recoup from campaigning! As soon as we're home you must come to Las Vegas! I want to see you! Alex and Molly want to see you, too! Hope all is well! Miss you!
Love,
Serena and Jonas

The number of exclamation points brought a smile to Jayne's lips. Serena lived life as if an exclamation point belonged after everything she did, whether at work or play, but she'd found her center with Jonas Benjamin, the newly elected mayor of Las Vegas. He absolutely adored his wife.

As soon as we're home you must come to Las Vegas!

Jayne wanted to see her friends, but she'd been putting off their invitations to visit. Venturing back to the neon-lit city, with its monstrous resorts and hundred-degree-plus temperatures, held little appeal and way too many memories of the time right after the breakup. Hmmm, maybe she could talk them into coming to San Diego instead. Her friends could bring their husbands and show the three men what their lives here had used to be like.

A life Jayne was still living.

She placed the postcard next to the plate of scones on the table and adjusted the book in her hands. Happily living, she reminded herself, even if her dreams had been put on hold and she was alone. Again.

She focused on the page, mentally taking notes on fresh ideas that might help the clients she counseled at the debt management center where she worked. No wonder the book had hit the bestsellers' list. The author had some great ideas for getting one's finances under control.

Several minutes later, the noise level in the teahouse increased exponentially, as if a crowd had entered all at once.

She looked up from the book, glanced behind her and saw a large group of women standing around and holding presents.

Her gaze collided with someone she recognized—Savannah Strickland, her ex-fiancé's youngest sister. A look of disbelief filled Savannah's hazel eyes before she turned away.

Was this a birthday party? Perhaps a baby shower for Grace, the oldest sister? Her third child must be due soon.

Curious, Jayne peeked at the colorfully wrapped presents. No bunnies. No duckies. No baby carriages. A few umbrellas, though.

Rich's other sister, Betsy, noticed Jayne, gasped and elbowed her twin, Becca. Both turned bright pink.

Jayne didn't understand their embarrassment. Sure this was a little awkward, considering what their brother had done to her, but his sisters weren't to blame for his...

Oh, no.

There she was.

Every single one of Jayne's nerve-endings stood at attention with a combination of shock and horror.

The other woman.

The reason Jayne was still single and her three friends were now married.

She forced her gaping mouth closed.

Jayne had only seen the woman once. At Rich's apartment. Days before their wedding. A living, breathing Barbie doll in lingerie.

Today, the woman's modest Wedgwood-blue dress and smart cap-sleeved white jacket were one hundred and eighty degrees from the black push-up bra with a bow at the center and the lace-trimmed leggings she'd worn at Rich's place. The pristine white headband securing long, straightened blonde locks was a far cry from the bed-tousled hair that had left no room for misinterpreting what had been going on between two consenting adults.

But it was *her*.

The woman's flushed cheeks were exactly the same.

And so were Jayne's feelings of betrayal.

Not a baby shower, she realized, stricken to the heart. A wedding shower.

Rich was getting married, and his sisters were throwing a bridal shower for the woman their brother had cheated on *her* with.

Jayne struggled to breathe.

Look away, she told herself. But, like a moth drawn to a flame, Jayne couldn't.

The scene was surreal and eerily familiar. A lot like her own bridal shower.

Tears stung her eyes. A lump formed in her throat.

How could his sisters bring *her* here? It was as if Jayne had never existed in their lives. As if she hadn't spent every Sunday having brunch at their parents' house or helped paint Grace's kids' bedrooms or a hundred other things Jayne had done with them.

For them.

For Rich.

Having him betray her was one thing—but his entire family, too?

Her stomach roiled. Jayne thought she might be sick.

Self-preservation instincts kicked in. Get out. Now.

She shoved her book into her purse, ripped out a twenty-dollar bill from her wallet and tossed the money on the table. The amount was double the cost of her tea and scones, but for once she didn't care about wasting a few dollars.

Jayne stood.

Someone called her name.

She cringed.

Not someone, but Grace, Rich's oldest sister—the one person in his family who'd called after the breakup to see how Jayne was faring.

Torn between what she wanted to do and what she should do, she looked over to see a very pregnant Grace. The concern in her eyes—eyes the same color and shape as Rich's—pricked Jayne's heart. She gave her almost-sister-in-law a pained, hesitant smile. That was all she could manage at the moment.

Grace moved awkwardly through the crowded room toward her.

No!

The air rushed from Jayne's lungs.

She had no idea what Grace wanted, but only one thing, one horrible thought, sprang to mind. No way could Jayne allow herself to be introduced to that woman. The other woman. The future Mrs. Rich Strickland.

A potent dose of anxiety fueled Jayne's already desperate panic. She mouthed *I'm sorry* to the fast approaching Grace, turned and fled.

The next day, Grace Strickland Cooper stood at the sink in her parents' kitchen after her family's weekly get-together for Sunday brunch. "I need a favor."

Must be his turn to wash. Tristan MacGregor stopped drying a saucepan and stared into the familiar brown eyes of his best friend's oldest sister. "If you leave your husband and two and three-quarter kids and run away with me, I'll do anything you ask."

Grace motioned with wet hands to her bulging baby-filled stomach. "Oh, yes. I'm exactly what an adventurous photo-journalist wants to wake up next to every morning."

"You're a beautiful woman. Any man would want to wake up next to you."

Her eyes narrowed. "I bet you say that to all the girls, pregnant or not."

"I will neither confirm nor deny." He hung the saucepan on one of the pot rack's hooks. "Though I usually try to stay away from the pregnant ones."

She shook her head. "You never change, MacGregor."

He flashed her his most charming grin. "But you still love me."

"In your dreams."

Tristan winked. "I'll take what I can get."

Laughing, she rinsed out a soapy pot. "I'm sure you have no problem getting whatever you want. You never did."

That had been true. At least until recently.

He avoided serious relationships, but he liked having fun. Lately he'd found himself comparing the women he met to an unattainable ideal. That was severely limiting his fun.

He picked up the towel and dried a frying pan. "So what do you need? Want me to take over washing?"

"No." She glanced around, as if to make sure they were still alone. "I saw Jayne Cavendish yesterday."

Hearing the name of Rich's ex-fiancée jolted Tristan from the inside out. He nearly dropped the pan. A big no-no, considering Mrs. Strickland's year-old marble countertops.

Jayne. His ideal woman…

A million questions sprang to mind. Not one could he ask. "Where?"

"She was at the teahouse where we had Deidre's shower. It was the same place we took Jayne, which must have made her feel even worse."

For Rich's sake Tristan had tried not to think about Jayne Cavendish, but she'd invaded his thoughts and taken over his dreams. She'd become the woman he measured all others against. He even carried her picture in his wallet.

"We were so embarrassed. I'd forgotten how much she liked the place," Grace continued. "Anyway, Jayne made a beeline for the exit before I could reach her."

"Do you blame her?" His words came out too harshly, given his role in the breakup.

"Not at all." Grace frowned. "I love my brother, but he acted like a complete jerk with Jayne. Rich should have broken off the engagement, not led her on the way he did after he met Deidre."

"I agree."

"But he didn't, and Jayne's the one who's suffered."

"Suffered?" Tristan hung the frying pan on a hook. "She should be relieved she didn't get married. Rich might be my best friend, but Jayne's better off without him."

"I call it as I see it." Grace dried her hands with a dishtowel, rummaged through her purse and handed him a postcard. "Jayne was in such a hurry to leave she forgot this at her table. I thought you could return it and check if she's doing okay."

See Jayne?

Tristan's heart pounded as if he'd stumbled across the perfect shot. No lighting or camera adjustment needed. Just point and click.

He'd wanted to see Jayne for months now, but two reasons kept him away: his travel schedule, and Rich. Speaking of which…

"Just call her," Tristan said.

"I can't," Grace admitted. "Deidre's feeling very insecure right now."

Not his problem. Rich had been so mad at Tristan for breaking his engagement. He didn't want to go through that again.

He returned the postcard to Grace. "Sorry, but I'm not sneaking behind Rich's back to do this."

"You wouldn't be sneaking behind his back." Grace shoved the postcard into Tristan's hand. "I figured there must be some kind of guy code you two follow, so I asked him about it when he arrived this morning."

"He's okay if I see Jayne?"

"Better you than me."

"Because I'm not family?"

Grace flushed. "You've been friends with my brother since you were toddlers. You're family. But Deidre really freaked out yesterday, so I told her I wouldn't have any contact with Jayne. There's no harm in you returning the postcard. Deidre won't feel as threatened if she finds out *you* saw Jayne. Everyone knows you didn't like her."

No one had a clue how Tristan felt about Jayne. "She and Rich weren't right for each other."

Staring at the soapy water in the sink, Grace shrugged. "Rich may have put Jayne behind him, but I can't forget about her and stop caring that easily."

"You didn't know her long."

"Length of time doesn't matter. She was going to be my sister-in-law and the baby's godmother. She even painted the kids' rooms for me. I can't help but think about her every time I'm in there." Grace placed her hands on her belly. Worry filled her eyes. "And when I saw Jayne yesterday, she seemed..."

Tristan's shoulder muscles knotted. "What?"

"Different," Grace said. "Jayne's lost weight. She's cut her hair short. But most of all she looked so sad. I guess that's normal under the circumstances. It's only been a few months since the breakup."

Seven months, one week and four days, Tristan thought.

"She probably shouldn't look like her cheerful self after everything that happened, but I can't help but worry about her." Grace drew her brows together. "Her parents are dead. She has no siblings. Jayne has no one to look out for her except her three best friends, and they weren't with her yesterday. She needs somebody, but it can't be me."

Rich's oldest sister had been Tristan's first crush years ago, but at this moment he loved Grace more than he ever had back when he'd been a kid. Her thoughtfulness had provided him with a valid reason to see Jayne Cavendish again. Not only a reason, but also permission from Rich.

Tristan could see if his attraction for Jayne was real or if he'd built her up in his mind because she was off-limits. He clutched the postcard as if it were a ticket to Shangri-la, even though his visit would probably be nothing more than a reality check for him.

"Stop worrying." He squeezed Grace's shoulder. "I'll head over there this afternoon, return the postcard and find out exactly how Jayne's doing."

"Thank you." Grace hugged him. Well, as much as she could hug given her beachball-sized belly. "And if you happen to know any nice single guys you could introduce her to…"

Tristan stiffened at the thought of Jayne with any of his friends. "One thing at a time, Grace."

Two hours later, Tristan noticed a California State Patrol car parked on the side of the 405 freeway and a radar gun pointed his way. He lifted his foot from the accelerator and tapped the brake pedal. Getting pulled over for speeding would only slow him down.

He gripped the leather-wrapped steering wheel as he passed the black and white police car. The officer didn't glance his way.

Good.

Tristan pressed down on the gas, making sure this time the speedometer didn't ease into get-a-ticket territory. He wanted to get to Jayne's.

She needs somebody, Grace had said, *but it can't be me*.

It shouldn't be him, either, but here he was, speeding—within safe limits, of course—to see Jayne.

Jayne Cavendish.

He remembered so much about her—the strawberry scent of her hair, the bubbly sound of her laughter and the warmth of her touch. Okay, one touch—a handshake—the very first time they'd met…

* * *

"Just because your marriage didn't work out—" Rich Strickland maneuvered his four-wheel drive pick-up truck into a spot at one of Balboa Park's parking lots "—doesn't mean mine won't."

"True." Still, Rich's fast approaching wedding date bothered Tristan—bothered him enough that he'd almost said no when his friend had asked him to be the best man. "But you weren't dating anyone when I left on assignment. I'm back a few months later, and now you're getting married in a couple of weeks. I don't understand the big rush."

"No rush." Rich removed the key from the ignition. "Jayne says when it's right it's right."

Tristan's concern ratcheted up three more notches. "Jayne says a lot."

Rich sighed. "Look, you're going to like her."

Maybe. Probably not.

But Tristan would refrain from saying more until he got to know her. That was one reason he'd given the couple a photoshoot around town as a wedding gift—to spend time with the woman who'd made his friend want to take the leap into domesticated hell, aka marriage.

"Give me some time to get used to the idea." Tristan stared at his blond-haired best friend. "I hate the idea of hitting the town without my wingman. That firefighter shtick you've got going is a real babe magnet."

"If it's any consolation, Jayne's friends are really hot," Rich said. "You might get lucky after the wedding."

Tristan wanted Rich to be the lucky one. He hoped his best friend's marriage turned out better than his had. Love, the forever kind at least, was as rare as a photograph of a rainbow's end. Rich's parents had found it, but few others. Tristan forced a smile. "That would be good."

"You mean great." Rich's cellphone rang. He glanced at the number. "I need to take this. I'll meet you by the fountain in the Rose Garden."

With a nod, Tristan grabbed his camera pack, exited the truck and entered Balboa Park along with a busload of German-speaking tourists. The park was home to museums, several gardens, and the San Diego Zoo.

He crossed the footbridge to the popular Rose Garden.

A breeze blew. The sweet scent of roses wafted in the air.

Tristan preferred taking pictures of people, not scenery. Faces, and especially eyes, told a story in a way landscape couldn't. A photographer took pictures of nouns—persons, places or things. A photojournalist captured verbs—action verbs—in a single image.

But the bursts of color coming from the circular tiered flowerbeds had him reaching for his camera anyway. His mother loved roses. He couldn't pass up this opportunity to take pictures for her, especially with her birthday next month.

As he moved toward the fountain, Tristan zoomed in on a nearby blossom—a lush orange rose that reminded him of the sky at sunset.

Satisfied he'd captured the image, Tristan looked around. An arbor covered with white roses. A gray-haired couple holding hands next to a yellow rosebush. And...

Pink.

Tristan did a double-take.

A tall, graceful figure stood among the full round blossoms. Her shirt was the same pale pink as the petals. She should have faded into the background, but she didn't. If anything, she seemed to be an extension of the flowers.

The play of light and shadow had him composing a long shot.

And what a shot.

Waist-length chestnut hair gleamed beneath the sun's rays like oiled teak, a complete contrast to the soft, warm shapes and pastel colors surrounding her.

Captivated by the scene, he took picture after picture.

She seemed oblivious to him, so he moved to shoot her from different angles. He drew closer for a medium shot, but that wasn't enough.

Tristan zoomed in on her face.

Large blue eyes framed by lush lashes focused on the delicate petals of a single rose. His pulse kicked up. He snapped a picture.

Full, pink-as-a-rosebud lips curved into a wide smile. His mouth wanted a taste of hers. He pressed the shutter button.

She bent to smell the rose. The scooped neckline of her shirt fell away, giving him a tantalizing view of ivory flesh and a white lace bra.

Nice—very nice.

And hot.

She straightened and smoothed her above the knee skirt.

Great long legs, too.

He widened the shot, squeezed off more photos and moved to intercept her. No way would he let this opportunity escape him.

Forget about asking for a model release. He wanted her.

"Hello," Tristan said.

Not exactly the most memorable of lines, but she'd rendered him speechless and short-circuited his brain. Rare feats. Ones he hadn't experienced in over a decade.

"Hi." Her sparkling blue eyes nearly knocked him off his feet. "I've been waiting for you."

Great line. Tristan didn't believe in love at first sight, but lust at first sight was another story. He curved his lips into a devastating grin—one that usually got him whatever he wanted. "I'm Tristan MacGregor."

"It's so nice to meet you." She stepped toward him, extended her arm and clasped his hand with hers. A burst of heat shot through his veins. "I'm Jayne Cavendish. Rich's fiancée."

CHAPTER TWO

Please pick up, please pick up, please pick up, please...

Sunday afternoon. Jayne tightened her grip on the phone receiver. She wanted to talk to someone about what had happened at the teahouse yesterday, but hadn't been able to reach any of her friends yet.

She paced across the living room.

How could she have not seen Rich for who he was?

But Jayne knew the answer. She'd let her desire for a happily-ever-after cloud her judgment. Never again.

Still, the familiar feeling of being a crumpled aluminum can tossed in the recycle bin was back. She'd been discarded, replaced by something else—someone better. If only she hadn't been so trusting, so naïve

The line clicked. Thank goodness.

"Hi. This is Molly. I can't get to the phone right now..."

Jayne's heart dropped to the tips of her bare feet.

No, no, no, no, no.

She didn't want to hear Molly's recorded voice. Jayne had already listened to Alex's cellphone message two hours ago. And she knew Serena was busy today.

A beep blared.

"Hey, Molly, it's me. Jayne," she added, as if one of her best friends and former roommate could have forgotten her name.

She winced. What a loser.

"Um. Call me when you get this. If…you know…you have time."

Jayne hit the "off" button and slammed the receiver in its charger.

Okay, that was totally pathetic. Nothing new, but pathetic just the same.

What was wrong with her?

Too bad Jayne knew the answer.

She needed to get out more. She needed to make new friends. She needed to get a life.

A twenty-eight-year-old woman needed more to fill her days than checking off items on her "To Do" list. Not that there was anything wrong with being home, but too much time alone wasn't good for her. Today was a prime example. She'd already organized her sock drawer, clipped the Sunday coupons and played enough games of Spider Solitaire to make her eyes cross. If she weren't careful, she'd wind up like her next-door neighbor, grandmotherly Mrs. Whitcomb, who loved to eavesdrop as she sat on her porch, and offered cookies to passersby in order to learn the latest gossip.

Jayne bit her lip.

Maybe she needed a hobby or a pet. She missed being welcomed home by Rocky, Molly's dog. A puppy would be too much work with Jayne's job, but a rescue dog—a housebroken one—might be a better choice. The yard was fenced. She'd have to talk with Molly, since this was her house, and see what she thought.

A knock at the door sounded.

Jayne's heart leaped.

She had no idea who it could be, but even a kid selling magazines to go to band camp would be a respite from the lonely quiet. She hurried across the gleaming hardwood floor, unlocked the deadbolt and whipped open the door. A tall, attractive man, dressed in a black T-shirt and faded blue jeans, stood on the "Welcome" mat.

Her mouth dropped open.

He was hot. Really hot. And vaguely familiar.

She pressed her lips together. In fact, he looked a little like… Just like… "Tristan?"

"Hello, Jayne."

His easy smile caught her like a softball under her ribs. She'd never expected to see Rich's best friend—his best man—again. In fact, she'd pretty much forgotten about Tristan MacGregor during the aftermath of the breakup. But now…

He seemed taller, his shoulders wider. Had he always had such intense green eyes?

Unwelcome awareness trickled through her. *Oh, my.*

His sun-streaked hair had grown longer. Whisker stubble covered his face. He should have looked scruffy, but Tristan didn't. With his long lashes, full, kissable lips and high cheekbones, he looked ruggedly handsome and dangerously sexy.

Jayne swallowed.

Not sexy. Bad-boy types didn't appeal to her. She preferred clean-cut, fresh-shaven, all-American types. Men like…

Rich.

He'd seemed so perfect—a handsome, stable firefighter, with a big family who all lived here in San Diego. But he hadn't been perfect. Far from it.

He'd let her down in every way possible, making her feel so stupid for rushing into the relationship and marriage. She hadn't spoken to her ex-fiancé since that night at his apartment. His last words to her had been, "Guess the wedding's off." He hadn't even given her the chance to break up with him. She'd received no explanation, no apology, nothing.

Now Rich's best friend was standing here. Alarms sounded in her head. "Why are you…?"

Tristan pulled something from a back pocket. Serena's postcard, Jayne saw with surprise. He handed it to her. "Grace asked me to return this to you."

"I must have forgotten it at the teahouse," Jayne said, thinking aloud. She rubbed her thumb along the edge of the postcard, remembering how quickly she had fled yesterday. "But why didn't Grace…?"

An image of Rich's oldest sister making her way across the tearoom flashed in Jayne's mind. Others, including his new fiancée, would have noticed.

"Grace couldn't come herself," Jayne said.

"She didn't want to upset Deidre."

Deidre. So that was *her* name.

Jayne couldn't believe Rich was already getting married when she hadn't even started dating again. Granted, he'd had a head start. Still, it seemed…wrong.

She took a deep breath and exhaled slowly. "I understand Grace has to put her family first. I wouldn't expect any less of her. She's always done the right thing for as long as I've known her."

Which hadn't been all that long, Jayne realized.

"Doing the right thing isn't always easy," Tristan said, as nosy, white-haired Mrs. Whitcomb exited the house next door and sat on her porch rocking chair. Her little dog Duke, a black and white Papillion, hopped on her lap.

Jayne waved at her elderly neighbor, who raised her cup of coffee in acknowledgement.

"Would you mind if we talked inside?" Tristan asked.

She took a quick, sharp breath. "You want to come in?"

He nodded.

"Um, sure."

But she wasn't sure about anything except for Mrs. Whitcomb's pastime of spying on neighbors. Jayne could only imagine what her neighbor would think of her inviting a strange, attractive man into the house, but she'd rather do that than talk within range of eager ears.

Tristan showing up out of blue left Jayne feeling off-balance. The guy had never been friendly or sought conversation with her. She didn't know why he wanted to start now. "If you really want to come in, okay, but please don't feel obligated. I mean, you returned the postcard. Mission accomplished."

"Actually, I wanted to talk to you," he said.

Apprehension coursed through her. She knew better than to trust a friend of Rich's. "Why?"

"Grace is worried about you."

Grace, huh? The tension knotting Jayne's shoulders eased slightly.

"Come in." She opened the door wider. "But you should know there's no reason for Grace to worry about me. I'm fine."

"Glad to hear it." His voice was low and smooth. "Then I won't have to waste a lot of your time."

"How is Grace doing?" Jayne asked. "It must almost be time for the baby to be born."

"Past time, but she's enjoying being with her other two kids, so she's happy."

"That sounds like Grace."

As Tristan walked past Jayne, the scents of earthy male and salt filled her nostrils. Quite a difference from the hyacinth potpourri she was used to smelling in the bungalow. She preferred the floral scent. "I appreciate you going out of your way to do this, but I'm sure you have somewhere else to be."

He stood in her living room, making the area feel cramped. "No, I'm free the rest of the day."

As she closed the door, Jayne hoped he didn't plan on staying long. Sure, she might have the company she'd been longing for, but Tristan wasn't who she had in mind. All she wanted was to get this visit over with. "Sorry you got roped into this by Grace."

"I'm not."

Jayne didn't know what to say to Tristan. She found herself glancing around the living room to avoid making eye contact with him. At least the house was clean—dusted, mopped and clutter-free. She'd done nothing but chores most of the weekend. That was what she did every weekend to keep busy.

Still, she couldn't be rude.

"Would you, um, like something to drink?" she asked. "A glass of iced tea, maybe?"

"That would be great," he said. "Thanks."

Jayne headed into the kitchen. She'd expected Tristan to wait in the living room, but he followed her instead.

No problem. He could see for himself that she was doing well and relay the information to Grace.

Except his six-foot plus frame took up a lot of space in the galley-style kitchen, making it hard for Jayne to maneuver without bumping into him. She noticed she'd left a bag of coffee on the counter—Kenyan roast: her favorite—and put it away.

"Need help?" he asked.

His offer surprised her. The guy looked as domesticated as a rampaging hippo. "Thanks, but I have it under control."

She wanted him to tell Grace that Jayne Cavendish had everything under control. No need to worry.

Tristan leaned against the counter and crossed his booted feet at the ankles. He might look out of place, but he sure acted comfortable—as if he were used to hanging out in women's kitchens.

He looked around. "I smell cookies."

His sense of smell was spot on. "I baked chocolate chip cookies this morning. Would you like one?"

"Please."

She reached for the plastic container full of cookies and placed a few on a plate. These homemade treats would give Tristan one more reason to tell Grace that Jayne Cavendish was fine and dandy.

Oh, no. She dropped a cookie onto the plate.

Forget fine. She wasn't dandy, either. She cringed.

She'd asked about Grace. Given the chance, Jayne would have asked about the other Stricklands, too. Maybe even Rich. She stared at the cookies with a sinking feeling in her stomach. She was turning into Mrs. Whitcomb.

Too late to renege on the offer of refreshments, but Jayne would not ask Tristan about another one of the Stricklands.

She would be polite. She would be gracious. But that was it.

With her resolve firmly in place, Jayne added ice to the two glasses, filled them with tea and handed one to Tristan.

He took a sip. "Sweet."

"Oops. I should have warned you," she said. "In the South, that's the only way they make it."

He considered her over his glass. "I don't hear an accent."

"I lived in North Carolina for a couple of years when I was younger." She remembered the humid summers, the enormous flying bugs, and missing her dad. "My father was in the military, so he was stationed all over the place."

"Lucky you." Tristan took another sip of his tea. "I was born in San Diego. My parents still live here."

"I'd say you're the lucky one." Jayne grabbed a few napkins. "I never want to move away from San Diego."

"It's a nice place to call home."

Too bad this place didn't feel like home at the moment. The kitchen was feeling a little too…crowded.

Jayne picked up the plate of cookies and her tea. "Let's go into the living room."

"After you."

In the living room, she placed the cookies on the scarred maple coffee table Molly had left when she moved to Las Vegas and pulled out two coasters for their glasses. Jayne sat on one end of the yellow plaid couch. "Tell me what you need to know to appease Grace."

And what it will take to get you out of here.

Tristan lowered himself onto the couch, making the full-sized sofa seem suddenly way too small. He set his glass on a coaster, adjusted a floral print pillow behind his back and stretched out—a mass of arms and legs. "Just a few things."

"Like what?"

As he placed his hand on the back of the sofa, his hand brushed Jayne's bare shoulder. Accidentally, of course.

Still, heat rushed down her arm like a lit fuse on a stick of dynamite.

She guzzled her tea, but the cold drink didn't cool her down at all. Even her fingertips seemed to sizzle.

Her reaction disturbed Jayne. It must be because she'd sworn off men. For the past seven months she'd barely seen a man outside of work, but the one sitting next to her on the overstuffed sofa was too warm, too solid, too…male. No wonder her body was so confused.

But being even the slightest bit attracted to Rich's best friend was a huge no-no.

She scooted away from Tristan until her hip collided with the sofa-arm. Darn. That wasn't far enough for her peace of mind.

He picked up a cookie. "Grace will want to know how you've been."

Add Rich's oldest sister to the list. Alex, Molly and Serena all kept asking how Jayne had been doing, so she wasn't surprised Tristan—make that Grace—would want to know, too.

"Please don't answer *fine*," he added. "You've already used that one."

Jayne usually answered *fine*. The word fit her most days—good or bad. She didn't want people worrying about her.

"I've been busy trying to make this house a home—my home, that is—when I'm not at the office," she said. "Everything is going…okay."

Okay seemed like the best, the safest answer. Because, face it, things might be fine, but they hadn't been great for a while now. Months, actually. She kept second-guessing herself. Something she had never done before. That had made things…harder.

He held his cookie in mid-air. "Okay, okay? Or okay, but I'd rather not talk about it?"

Her gaze met his. She hadn't expected him to delve further or to read so much into her simple answer. "A little of both."

"An honest answer."

She raised her chin. "I'm an honest person."

"Honesty is a rare quality these days."

"No kidding." Jayne wasn't about to disagree with him, especially after her experience with Rich. The cheating jerk.

And what did that say about Tristan? He and Rich were best friends.

She watched a bead of condensation drip down her glass.

"You cut your hair," Tristan said.

Her gaze met his. "I'm surprised you noticed."

"I'm a photographer, remember?" he said, as if that explained anything. "An eye for detail."

She'd forgotten. Her cheeks burned. How could she have forgotten what he did for a living? He'd spent two days trailing her and Rich around town, taking their picture. But then again, she'd pushed as much of that painful time out of her memory as possible. That included her groom's best man.

Still, she wanted to cover her embarrassment.

"My friends treated me to a makeover at a fancy salon in Las Vegas." She fingered the short ends. "Rich told me never to cut my long hair, so I told the stylist to chop it all off. I had a moment of sheer panic when she did, but decided I actually liked the shorter length and have kept it this way even though there are times I look in the mirror and don't recognize myself."

Tristan drew his brows together.

Uh-oh. Deep in thought? Or disgusted by her rambling? Not that his opinion mattered to her. "Too much information?"

"Not at all," he said. "I was just looking at your hair. The longer length was nice, but this style flatters your features better. You should get your picture taken."

Thinking about the deposit she'd lost canceling the wedding photographer sent a shiver down her spine. Of course she'd lost a lot more than money with the breakup. Pride. Respect. Confidence. "I don't like having my picture taken."

"I remember." His lips formed a wry grin. "But I managed to get some good shots anyway."

"I never saw any of them."

"I'll get you copies."

Jayne crossed her arms over her chest. "Um, I…"

"Bad memories?" Tristan guessed.

"Yeah, sorry, but thanks for the offer." She picked up a cookie. "I know Rich is your best friend, but he wasn't the man I thought he was. I wouldn't want to spend the rest of my life with someone like him."

Even if she'd thought he could give her everything she'd wanted. Everything, that was, except his love and fidelity.

Dredging up the past made her uncomfortable. This called for chocolate. She bit into her cookie.

"Then everything worked out for the best," Tristan said.

Still chewing, she nodded.

"You'll find someone else," he said. "Someone better."

Jayne choked, coughed, and reached for her tea. Plunging back into the dating scene was about as appealing as a case of food poisoning. Taking a year off from dating seemed a reasonable amount of time after a broken engagement. She needed time to regain the self-confidence to make the right decisions and trust her judgment again.

Besides, her three friends had found the loves of their lives when they hadn't been trying to find "the one." Maybe Jayne had been going about this happily-ever-after business the wrong way. Maybe she'd been trying too hard to get what she wanted. "I'm not really looking."

"You don't have to look. Someone will find you."

Her breath caught in her throat. Tristan sounded so...romantic—a way she'd never heard him sound in the short time she'd known him. He'd always seemed so unfriendly, almost arrogant, back then.

"You won't have to do anything," he added.

Her heart melted a little. That sure would be nice.

Thanks to what had happened to her best friends in Las Vegas, Jayne knew Mr. Right finding her could happen. And she really did want it to happen one of these days.

Ever since she was a little girl Jayne had wanted the fairytale to come true. She was over the heartbreak Rich had caused, but she wanted to focus on work and getting her life back in order first. Her heart had fooled her. She didn't want to be duped again.

"I hope that happens *someday*." She emphasized the final word. "Just because things with Rich didn't work out doesn't mean I can't live happily ever after here in San Diego with my one true love."

"If that's what you want, go for it."

She thought about her and her mother's dream. "Isn't that what everybody wants?"

Tristan set his iced tea on the table. "Not me."

Okay, so maybe the guy wasn't so romantic after all. She shouldn't be surprised, given his long-time friendship with Rich. A true romantic wouldn't condone a cheater's behavior. "That sounds a little...bitter."

"Not bitter, just experienced." He stared at his glass. "I gave marriage a try. It didn't work out."

She leaned toward him. "You were married?"

He nodded. "You sound surprised."

"I am," she blurted. He was attractive enough to have his pick of female companionship, yet had chosen to settle down. She wondered what kind of woman had made him want to say *I do*. No doubt a gorgeous model or actress-type, with a killer body. "I mean, you don't seem like the marrying kind."

"I realized I'm not, but I tried to make it work."

Yeah, right. That was what all men said, but actions spoke louder than words. If only she'd realized that with the first man in her life…her father.

Her dad had done nothing to make things work with her mother. Jayne still remembered hearing her parents' yelling late at night when she'd be in bed. Still, she'd never thought he'd leave one day and never contact her again. "Let me guess—you were misunderstood?"

Tristan laughed. "No, she understood me quite well. I take full responsibility for the failure of my marriage."

His words touched Jayne. Her father had never admitted failure. He'd blamed all their problems on her mother. God rest her soul. "That must be a hard thing to admit."

"I'm just being honest."

"I appreciate that," she said. "As you said, honesty is a rare quality these days."

One she hadn't expected from Tristan MacGregor.

"Have you been married before?" he asked.

"No, my parents were divorced, so I told myself to make sure it was right first and not rush into anything."

"Until Rich."

She nodded. "I didn't follow my own advice with him, and rushed in with my eyes full of stars, but I won't do that again."

Jayne looked at the table. Only crumbs remained on the cookie plate. Her glass was empty. Tristan's was only a quarter full. By now he should see she was fine and be able to reassure Grace. Nothing left to do but say goodbye. Except…

He didn't seem in any hurry to finish his iced tea and leave.

"Anything else you want to know so you can tell Grace?" Jayne asked, trying to move him along. "I hate keeping you here."

"You're not keeping me." His gaze took in the knickknacks on the bookcase and the framed photographs on the fireplace mantel. "It's nice be in a house. I just got back from two months in Malaysia and Bali."

Two months? That would have included last month... December. "You were overseas for Christmas?"

He nodded. "You can celebrate Christmas anywhere."

But it wasn't the same as being home. Not that Christmas alone here had been all that great. Still, she'd had a small tree and presents sent by her friends—including a filled stocking.

"I can't imagine being on the go so much." Just the thought gave Jayne the heebie-jeebies. She rubbed her arms. "Away for weeks or months at a time. I get tired thinking about it."

"I get more tired when I'm *not* traveling," he admitted. "If I'm in one place too long I get antsy."

She'd heard that so many times. "My father was like that."

"What about you?"

"I take after my mother," Jayne said with pride. "I traveled so much when I was younger there's no place I want to go now. I'm pretty much a homebody."

Tristan's eyes narrowed. "You don't seem like a homebody."

"You just don't know me that well. Growing up, I was always bugging my parents for a house with a yard and a puppy."

"You want a dog?"

"Maybe." She shrugged. "My former roommate had a dog. I walk my neighbor's dog most evenings. But I'm still debating whether this place needs a pet or not."

"It's a nice place."

"Thanks," she said. "I lucked out getting to live here."

"How's that?" Tristan asked.

"Well, I'd given notice on my studio apartment to move in with Rich after the wedding, so I found myself homeless after he—I mean we—broke up. My friend Molly had a spare bedroom and told me to move in with her. It was only supposed to be a temporary arrangement, but she fell in love with a man she met during a girls' weekend in Las Vegas, married him a few months later, and relocated to Sin City. And that's how I ended up with this charming bungalow to call home."

"You did luck out."

Jayne nodded. "Though I liked having Molly for a roommie. I miss talking to her late at night over a pint of Ben & Jerry's."

"So find a new roommate. Preferably one who likes ice cream."

A new roommate. Jayne thought about his suggestion. Someone to talk to. Someone to split the rent and utilities with. "You know, Tristan, getting a roommate is a really good idea."

"Unless you prefer living alone."

"I don't like being alone," she answered quickly. "I mean, Molly and my other two best friends have moved away. With the three of them gone it's been a little…"

Loser, Jayne thought. When would she learn to keep her mouth shut and not say so much?

"Lonely?" he finished for her.

"Yes," she admitted, wishing she'd put more cookies out.

"You lost your fiancé and your three best friends."

She nodded. "The only two things that haven't changed in the last seven months are my job and my car."

"That's tough."

"It's been…challenging."

He scooted closer. "I guess it has."

Oh, no, she thought. He was Rich's friend. And here she was babbling about her life and sounding really pathetic. What if Tristan told Rich?

Her insides clenched. She couldn't bear the thought of that happening.

"Not that I'm unhappy with the way things turned out," she added hastily.

"Glad to hear it."

Tristan shifted position. His leg touched hers. No skin-on-skin contact was made, but warmth emanated from the spot. Worse, his jean-clad leg remained pressed against hers.

Maybe he didn't notice, but she sure did.

Unfortunately she couldn't move. The sofa-arm blocked her in one direction, Tristan in the other. She was…trapped.

The only thing she could do was ignore it. Him. "I wonder how hard finding a roommate would be."

"You can't beat this location." As he looked around the living room, she prayed he would notice his leg was still touching her. "And you keep the place nice. Neat. It'll all depend on the room."

Companionship and only paying half her current living expenses sounded like an ideal combination. Why hadn't she thought of getting a roommate herself?

"Oh, the room is lovely. It's not that large, but has lots of windows."

"Show me," Tristan said.

"Sure." Jayne jumped up, eager to get away from the intimacy of the couch. She led him past her room into the other bedroom. "This used to be Molly's room."

"Great room." He checked the closet. "Why didn't you take this one for yourself?"

"The two bedrooms are almost the same size, and I didn't want to move."

"Across the hall?"

"My room is decorated the way I like it."

He looked out one of the large windows facing the backyard garden. "Nice view."

His position gave her a view of his backside. His faded jeans fit well. "Very nice."

What was she *doing*? With cheeks burning, she looked away.

"You'll have no trouble renting this room out," he said.

The thought of not being alone all the time made Jayne wiggle her toes. Maybe something good would come from Tristan's impromptu visit. "I better put together an ad."

Tristan turned toward her with his brows drawn together. "You're serious about this?"

She heard the surprise in his voice. She was a little surprised herself, but loneliness could drive a person to do some crazy things. "Yes, and it'll give me something to do this afternoon." Jayne winced when she realized how her words must have sounded. "I mean—"

"Forget the ad," Tristan interrupted. "Spending the rest of this beautiful afternoon inside would be a crime."

Yes, but she didn't have anything else to do, and the last thing she wanted was his pity. She didn't want anything to do with him.

She raised her chin. "I happen to like staying home."

"That's okay, but you should get out more."

Going out alone had gotten old fast. She shrugged.

"Let's go on a hike," he said.

Her heart picked up speed. "A hike?"

"Yes." Mischief gleamed in his eyes. "The fresh air will be good for a homebody."

"Why would you want to go on a hike with me?" She felt as if she'd entered an alternative universe. One where everything had flipped upside down and inside out. "You don't like me."

Tristan jerked as if she'd slapped him. "I like you."

"No, you don't."

"Yes, I do."

"The only reason you're here is for Grace."

"Grace asked me to stop by, but that doesn't mean I don't want to be here."

Jayne didn't—couldn't—believe him. Her assessing gaze raked over him.

No way was he telling her the truth.

"Have you forgotten the way you acted toward me before the breakup?" His unfriendly behavior had gotten worse each time she saw him. "It was pretty obvious to everyone—including Rich," she added, as if that was the clincher. As if Rich's judgment could be trusted. As if *Rich* could be trusted, the lying rat.

Tristan's dark eyes locked with hers. "Everyone, including Rich, is wrong."

The words hung in the air, as if suspended in a floating bubble.

Wrong.

Emotion tightened Jayne's throat.

She'd never understood why Tristan had behaved the way he had. *Could* she be wrong? She wanted to believe him. Which made her mistrust her own judgment even more. She wasn't a good judge of character when it came to men. Taking a man at his word, even when he said he loved you, was a huge mistake. One she'd made with her father and with Rich. Trust had to be earned, not given.

Tristan rocked back on his heels. "Come on. It'll be fun."

Fun. When had that word become an alien concept? Maybe…

No.

Tristan MacGregor wasn't some attractive stranger inviting her for a walk. He was Rich Strickland's best friend. His best man. She'd have to be out of her mind to go anywhere with Tristan. Out of her mind or very, very lonely.

Her own thought ricocheted through her brain.

Loneliness could drive a person to do some crazy things.

She swallowed a sigh.

"What do you have to lose?" Tristan asked.

Nothing. Jayne's shoulders had started to sag, but she squared them instead. She'd already lost everything.

Her fiancé, her trust, her hope, her three best friends.

Life had become one lonely hour followed by another. She rarely left the house, and when she did she couldn't wait to get home.

Just like her mother.

The unsettling realization made Jayne straighten.

Her mother had stuck close to home after her father had left. She'd gone to work, the store, and occasionally to church. She hadn't even wanted to go to the doctor's office when she'd started feeling poorly, and because of that she'd ended up dying way too soon.

Jayne didn't want that to happen to her.

Something had to change. *She* had to change. Now.

Maybe one small step—one short hike—would start her on a new road…a path toward the life she wanted to live, not the one she was living. Even if the hike *was* with the last person, next to Rich, she wanted to spend time with.

"You're right," she said finally. "A hike will do me good."

CHAPTER THREE

"HIKING has been good for me—" Jayne puffed behind Tristan "—but I don't know how much further I can go."

He turned on the trail, happy to be finally spending time with her. She might not be exactly the woman he remembered, but the woman he was getting to know intrigued him.

She closed the distance between them. Her feet dragged—something they hadn't done at the start of the hike. But even tired, flushed and sweaty, with her hair sticking out of that old San Diego Padres baseball cap she wore, she was still the best thing he'd seen in weeks…maybe months.

"We're almost to the beach," he said.

She adjusted the brim of her hat. "Okay, then. I guess I can make it."

"Sure you can." But Tristan didn't want to wear her out before they reached their destination. He opened his water bottle. "I need a drink first."

Relief filled her pretty eyes. "That sounds good to me, too."

Talk about a good sport. Tristan took a swig of water. He liked that about her.

Despite an extended and thoughtful moment of hesitation back at her apartment, she'd gamely accepted his invitation to go hiking at Torrey Pines State Park. She hadn't once complained about the hot afternoon sun blazing down on them even though it was only January.

Jayne drank from her water bottle. Her pink tongue darted out to lick the liquid off her lips.

He took another gulp from his bottle.

She sure was a nice addition to the already beautiful scenery surrounding them. Her legs, exposed between the hem of her khaki shorts and hiking books, looked long and slim and smooth. The sky intensified the blue of her eyes. A hint of a smile tugged at the corners of her glossed lips.

Tristan put away his water bottle and focused his camera on her.

Jayne pretended to scowl. "Again?"

He preferred her mock exasperation to the loneliness he'd glimpsed earlier at her apartment. "Just capturing memories."

Lines creased her forehead. "Memories of a day spent with a stranger?"

Her suspicious tone bothered him. "We're not strangers."

"We aren't friends."

"We could be friends," he countered.

She pursed her lips. "Why are you being so nice to me?"

Because he liked her. He wanted her to like him. But she wasn't ready to hear that.

In her wary eyes he was still only Rich's best man. Rich's best friend. And Rich had let her down big time.

"You're a nice person," Tristan answered.

"Nice, huh?"

He nodded.

"The last time we were together you didn't even look me in the eye."

Tristan remembered. He wasn't as nice as Jayne was. But even a jerk would have had trouble looking a bride straight in the eye when he knew her fiancé was two-timing her with another woman.

Tristan aimed at the basket. Swoosh. Two points.

"Lucky shot," Rich said, taking away the ball.

The two had been co-captains of their high school basketball team and won two district titles. Whenever Tristan was in town they would shoot hoops at the gym.

"Next time it'll be for three," he said.

Rich dribbled the ball and scored with a lay-up. "You'd better hope so."

A cellphone rang. Rich's. For the third time in the past hour. For the third time he ignored it.

"You want to get that?" Tristan asked.

"Nah. Probably just Jayne."

Tristan held the ball. "I'll wait."

"No. She keeps bugging me about the wedding." Rich rolled his eyes. "Everything's about the wedding with her."

"Your wedding, too, buddy."

"You're sticking up for her?" Rich asked.

"No, but remember how Grace and Becca turned into Bridezillas before they got married?"

No answer. Something was up.

"Tell me what's going on," Tristan said.

Rich started, then stopped himself.

"Come on." Tristan passed the ball hard at Rich's chest. "It's me."

Rich looked around, as if to make sure no one else was there. "I met someone."

Tristan got a sinking feeling in his gut. "A female someone?"

Rich nodded and tossed the ball back. "She's a dental hygienist and totally hot. Smokin'."

"So is Jayne." Okay, maybe Tristan shouldn't have said that about his best friend's bride to be, but Rich didn't appear to notice. He was still going on about this other girl. Deidre Something.

Annoyance flared.

Cold feet or not, Rich was being an idiot. Time to call him on it.

"You can't drill your dentist, bud." Tristan dribbled the basketball. The sound echoed through empty gymnasium. "What did she do? Put the moves on you in the chair?"

"She was in a car accident we responded to." Rich glanced around the empty court again like a man being watched. Or one who didn't want to get caught. "A few days later she brought brownies to the station and invited me to dinner. I couldn't say no."

Rich could have said no, but he hadn't wanted to. Not good.

Tristan spun the ball in his hands. "So you screwed up one time? You're engaged. Just tell her."

"It was more than once," Rich admitted. "And I'm not telling her about Jayne. Deidre wouldn't see me anymore."

"She's not going to see you anymore anyway, bonehead. You're getting married in a week."

"I know, but… Hell, I think I'm in love with her. Deidre," Rich clarified.

Tristan dropped the ball. "What? Are you kidding? What about the wedding?"

"I'm sick of thinking about the wedding. That's all Jayne can talk about. All she sees. Deidre treats me like I'm the best thing that ever happened to her. The most important thing in her life."

"Probably because you saved her life," Tristan countered, wanting, needing to say something. Anything. An image of Jayne, bright-eyed and smiling, flashed in his mind. He couldn't believe Rich was doing this to her. "It's a crush. Deidre will get over it."

"Maybe I don't want her to get over it. Maybe I like being somebody's hero."

Damn. Tristan thought for a minute. "How long has this been going on?"

"Not long," Rich admitted. "A couple of weeks, maybe."

"You've got to talk to Jayne."

Rich stared at Tristan as if he'd grown antennae and a third eye. "Why?"

"You can't get married if you're in love with someone else."

"I'm not canceling the wedding." Rich set his jaw. "I asked Jayne to marry me, and I will marry her."

Uh-oh. Tristan knew that mulish tone of Rich's all too well. "What about Deidre?"

"I'm trying to figure that out."

"Better figure it out fast, because you can't have both."

"I know." Rich looked miserable. "Look, just don't… Don't say anything to Jayne. Promise me you won't."

Tristan had kept his mouth shut. But his guilt over knowing the truth had made it difficult for him to face Jayne the next time he saw her, and each time after that. He'd thought by ignoring her he would buy Rich the time he needed to make the right decision.

Wrong.

Rich had ignored the matter, forcing Tristan to keep his best friend and Jayne from getting married. He didn't regret his actions one bit. But dragging up the past and telling Jayne what he'd done to engineer her discovering Rich's cheating now wouldn't help anyone. She'd admitted she wouldn't have wanted to marry Rich. She was moving on. Rich was getting married. Tristan was finally getting to spend time with Jayne. It was better to bury the past.

"It wasn't you," Tristan said finally.

The doubt in her big blue eyes hit him right in the gut.

You don't like me.

The problem was he did like her.

He'd always liked her.

Too much.

And for that reason he'd kept his distance from her and limited his contact with her. Even after the breakup. For all their sakes.

Yet he was here now, and he wouldn't want to be anywhere else.

"It was me," he finished.

She smiled crookedly. "Yeah, that's what the guy always says."

He winced. "I'm...sorry."

"Hey," she said. "I'm sorry for putting you on the spot like this."

"No worries."

Her closed-mouth smile turned into a wide grin. His pulse kicked up.

Man, she really had a great smile. He took another picture of her.

"Knock it off," she said, but her eyes gleamed with laughter.

"Professional photographer, remember?" A gull flew overhead, its sharp white wings contrasting with the cloudless blue sky. He turned his camera from her to the bird. "It's an occupational hazard."

"I'd say it's more a hazard for anyone who happens to be around you."

"Having your photograph taken isn't a hazard."

"Some cultures believe being photographed steals a part of your soul."

"I'm not a soul-stealer," he said. "I'm only after the image. The best photographs tell a story, and can often be described by a single verb."

She took another slug from her water bottle. "Well, as long as you aren't stealing souls, I suppose it's okay, but please don't go overboard."

He gave a mock bow. "Your understanding is much appreciated, since my camera follows me everywhere. No questions asked."

"Sounds like a perfect relationship for you."

"It is," he admitted. "My camera packs light, doesn't hog the bed, and never gets upset when I don't remember its birthday."

"Men."

"We are what we are."

A breeze caught the ends of her hair. He snapped her picture again.

She sighed.

"I'm not going overboard," he said.

"Just make sure you delete the bad ones."

Tristan feigned innocence. "You mean I can't post them on the internet?"

She grimaced.

He laughed. "I'll delete the bad ones. Scouts' Honor."

"A Boy Scout, huh?" Jayne studied him. "I'm not seeing it."

"My Scout days were brief," he said. "I was more interested in spying on girls than lighting a fire with flint and learning first aid techniques. Though the orienteering I learned saved my neck in Afghanistan, so it wasn't a total waste."

"You were over there?"

He nodded. "Iraq, too. Gotta be where the action is to get the good shots."

Biting her lower lip, she stared off in the distance.

Tristan looked through his viewfinder in the same direction. He focused his camera on the weathered and wrinkled hills full of caverns, caves and creases. Beyond them, a sea of blue stretched to the horizon.

"Interesting geography," she said softly. "I didn't realize the coast had badlands."

He snapped a picture of the scenery. "I thought everyone who lived in San Diego had been here before."

"Not me," she said. "This is the second time I've lived in San Diego, but the first time I was only six, so the Zoo and Sea World were on the top of my must-see list."

Tristan glanced her way. "Sounds like you need to play tourist as an adult."

"Maybe I do," she said.

"Homebodies aren't us."

"Even homebodies need breaks."

Now that was more like it. Her eyes were brighter. Her color was better. "Well, Ms. Homebody, ready to head to the beach?"

She nodded.

"Lead the way."

Jayne glanced down the trail and then up uncertainly at his face. "I suppose with the beach as our final destination it would be hard to get lost."

"Nearly impossible."

"Okay, let's go." She headed down the trail.

As he followed her, the sound of waves crashing against the shore became more distinct.

"The view is incredible," she said.

Tristan agreed. He really appreciated the view of Jayne's swaying hips in front of him.

A family of five going in the opposite direction passed them on the trail. A harried, sweat-soaked dad wore a backpack with a wiggling kid inside. A sunburned mom trudged uphill, holding the hands of two little girls, dressed in matching pink outfits and sunhats, each of whom wanted to go their own way.

Jayne glanced up the trail as the family continued on toward the top of the bluff. "Cute kids. I bet they had fun out here."

"The parents didn't look like they were having fun. More like they were in need of alcohol and lots of it."

"I'm sure they have their hands full with those three."

"Better them than me."

"Don't you like kids?" she asked.

He shrugged. "I'm an only child. I don't have a lot of experience with kids except for Grace's brood."

"I'm an only, too." Jayne got a wistful look on her face. "I would like to have a big family."

Tristan imagined her leading a child with one hand and holding a baby in the other. She would be a good mom.

"You coming?" Jayne called from a few feet ahead of him.

He shook the disturbing image of her from his head. A wife and kids were not in his future. No way, no how. He'd never had any desire to take family portraits for a living; he sure as hell didn't want to be in one. "I'm right behind you."

Continuing down the trail, she made her way through the sandstone-lined entrance to the wet sand beach where waves crashed against the shore.

She stared up at the walls of eroded sandstone. "Wow."

Wow was right. The look of awe on her face tightened his chest. She seemed so young and vulnerable next to the weathered old rock. He took her picture.

She gave him a look.

He didn't care. "Some day you'll thank me for capturing these moments."

"You think?"

He shrugged. "Time will tell."

Jayne stared up at him with a puzzled expression on her face.

His answer seemed to catch her off-guard, but she looked damn adorable right now. He wanted to kiss her soft, moist lips and watch the confusion in her eyes turn to passion.

He'd wanted to kiss her from the first moment he'd seen her, but doing so now would be a bad move.

She was sending out no signs that she wanted to be kissed.

If she did he would be all over it. Over her.

Tristan smiled at the thought. "Ready to explore the beach?"

* * *

Exploring the beach with Tristan showed Jayne a different side of him. With his camera in hand and a smile on his face he seemed as carefree as one of the gulls flying over the water. So different from when he'd photographed her and Rich.

But, however relaxed, Tristan was still Rich's best friend. No way could she let her guard down. Not even for a minute.

She followed Tristan back to his car. Her thighs burned. She tugged on the straps of her daypack.

"Need help?" he asked.

"I've got it, thanks."

Jayne removed her pack, unlaced her boots and took off her socks. She placed everything on the floor of the backseat, as Tristan had done. She slid into the front seat, where her sandals were waiting for her, fastened her seatbelt and relaxed against the car's leather seat.

It felt so good to sit. She almost sighed.

Tristan placed the key in the ignition. "How about a bite to eat?"

The idea appealed to her. She didn't relish the thought of returning to an empty apartment, but she'd spent enough time with him today. "No, thanks."

He started the engine. "Aren't you hungry?"

Surprisingly, she was. She'd wondered if her appetite would ever return or not. Maybe she should take up hiking as her hobby. "Yes, but I'm sweaty, dirty, and not dressed to go out."

His gaze lingered on her shirt that stuck to her skin. "You look fine to me."

She couldn't imagine he was flirting with her, but still she crossed her arms over her chest. "Thanks, but—"

"What sounds good?" he interrupted. "Thai? Mexican? Italian?"

"Mexican, but—"

"I know just the place."

Half an hour later Jayne found herself seated across from Tristan at a small table for two while a Mariachi band played outside on the tiled courtyard. She stretched her tired legs. Her feet bumped Tristan's. The material of his jeans brushed her calf for the second time in less than five minutes.

"Sorry," she mumbled.

"No worries," he said.

Maybe not for him, but the quickening of her pulse had nothing to do with the hiking they'd done earlier. She curled her feet beneath her chair so she wouldn't end up touching him again. "The table's a little crowded."

"Cozy," he corrected.

Cozy was the last thing she wanted. Jayne downed her glass of ice water. Cozy implied romantic. No way did she want this dinner to be romantic at all.

That begged a question.

What was she doing having dinner with a guy who happened to be her ex-fiancé's best friend?

Jayne eyed the full basket of corn tortilla chips and the small bowl of *pico de gallo* salsa. Better to look at the food than at Tristan. He had enough appreciative stares from the other females in the restaurant. Surely he had better things to do on a Sunday than spend time with her?

"You're quiet," he said.

Because she was thinking about him. No way could she admit that aloud. Serena probably would have, but not Jayne. "Just taking it all in after the long hike."

A busboy, wearing all white and carrying a silver pitcher, refilled her water glass.

She thanked him as he walked away. "I have no doubt I'll be sore tomorrow. A good sore."

Tristan reached for a chip. "Fresh air and exercise are good for the soul."

"Well, I definitely needed both."

"And company."

It wasn't a question. Jayne met his gaze. She cleared her dry throat. "That, too."

He smiled at her.

Easy, charming.

She didn't trust charm.

She didn't trust him.

She couldn't trust him.

He was Rich's friend, after all.

Still, Jayne couldn't deny there was something pleasant about sitting across a restaurant table from a handsome man who looked at her with appreciation in his eyes and a smile on his lips. Much better than, say, heating a frozen entrée in her microwave and eating in an empty house alone. That was where she'd be if Tristan hadn't taken matters into his own hands.

"Do you always get your way?" she asked.

"Usually, but in this case it was for your own good."

"How do you figure that?"

"You looked hungry."

"Well, I am now," she admitted. "So thanks."

"You're welcome." He raised his water. "That's what friends are for."

"Is that what we are? Friends?"

"We could be."

Jayne couldn't imagine her and Tristan ever being friends. Not the kind of friend you called late at night when your car wouldn't start or some guy had broken your heart. He looked more like a heartbreaker than a best bud or best friend forever.

He scooted back in his chair. The movement caused strands of his hair to fall forward across the right side of his face. He really was attractive. Okay, gorgeous.

She fought the urge to push the locks away so she'd have a better view of his eyes. She liked how his green irises seemed to change shade with his emotions. A vibrant jewel-like color when excited. A lighter, more subdued one when thoughtful. She wondered what the color looked like when he kissed.

Uh-oh. That wasn't a very friend-like thought. Not that they *were* friends. Jayne shoved a chip into her mouth.

A waiter, wearing a long-sleeved white shirt, black pants and a colorful sash around his waist, placed dinner plates in front of them and walked away. The scents of cilantro, tomatoes and chili peppers brought a sigh to her lips.

"Good call on Mexican food tonight," Tristan said.

"It's one of my favorites." Though she couldn't remember ever having such a strong reaction to food before. Her mouth practically watered as she stared at her plate of Chile Rellenos, refried beans and rice.

"Mine, too." Tristan picked up his fork. "It's the first thing I want to eat when I get back into town. Good Mexican food is hard to find."

"My dad used to say the same thing, but my mom never had any luck using that argument to convince him to make San Diego their home base when they were married," she said. "That was her dream. To live here again. But she never got the chance."

"You're living the dream for her?"

Jayne straightened. "I am."

And one of these days she'd fulfill the rest of the dream they'd talked about over the years.

Tristan dug into his Chile Colorado. "Eat up."

She did.

As they ate, they quizzed each other on favorites—television shows, movies, sporting teams. Their tastes converged, diverged, and found common ground with the San Diego Padres and Chargers.

Jayne scooped up the last forkful of rice. "I can't believe I ate everything. I haven't had this much of an appetite in months."

"Seven months?"

She nodded. "In case you're wondering, I'm over Rich. It just takes time for things to get back to normal. At least that's what Molly told me. She said you can't rush it."

"She's right."

"Molly is usually right," Jayne said. "She was divorced a couple of years ago, but she's remarried and expecting her first baby. All because of our weekend in Las Vegas."

"Sounds like a wild time."

Jayne blew out a puff of air. "You have no idea."

"Tell me about it."

"I wouldn't know where to start," she admitted. "I mean, my three best friends ended up with husbands because of that one weekend. Alex received a job offer and never came back to San Diego. She ended up falling in love with her boss, Wyatt. Molly met Linc while having a glass of wine in a hotel lounge, and that led to—well, a baby and marriage. Then there's Serena, who met Jonas at a bar and ended up marrying him that night."

"And you?"

"Well, I was in my hating-men phase then. I wanted nothing to do with any of the pondscum-sucking species. No offense."

"None taken."

Jayne fluffed the ends of her hair. "So I came home with a new 'do instead."

"A lot less of a commitment than a husband or a baby."

"Most definitely."

"You made the right choice."

The relief in his voice surprised her. Jayne studied him. "You really don't want to get married again?"

"I don't."

"Even after everything I went through with Rich I can't imagine growing old on my own. Celebrating a fifty-year anniversary just sounds so right."

"To you, maybe," he said. "I'd consider that a life sentence."

"It's one I'd happily serve." When she found the right man—a trustworthy man. The last thing she wanted to do was be swept off her feet by another Mr. Wrong.

The waiter placed the bill on the table.

Tristan reached for the black vinyl folder.

She grabbed hold at the same time. "No."

"Guy rules." He pulled the check toward him. "The guy pays for the date. Especially the first date."

Jayne tugged on the bill. "But this isn't a date."

He started to speak, then stopped.

"You're right. It's not a date." Tristan let go. "Let's split the check."

"Thanks." Jayne opened the folder, added a twenty percent tip and divided the total in half. With her purse open, she removed the envelope with "Eating out" written in black marker and counted out in cash the exact amount she owed. She tucked the money inside the folder. "Here's my half."

"What's with the envelope?" Tristan asked.

"It's a way to keep track of your spending money when using cash."

Tristan tossed a platinum-colored credit card into the folder. "I prefer using plastic for everything and earning frequent flier miles."

"Don't you earn enough miles with your job travels?" she asked.

"I use the mileage for my personal travels," he said.

Jayne didn't understand why a person would want to be away from home that much, or use a credit card that way, but she bit her tongue. Tristan wasn't one of those clients who needed to hear her spiel about the dangers of relying and living off credit. Or how much interest people ended up paying to get a "free" plane ticket or a minuscule cashback reward.

"Besides, credit cards are more convenient than cash," he added.

"Convenient?" Oops. She hadn't meant to say that aloud. She pressed her lips together and counted to ten, the way Alex always did. It didn't help. "You may think credit cards are convenient, but only until you find yourself in debt with collection agencies stalking you."

"Huh?"

"I'm a debt management counselor," she said. "Everyday I help people get their finances under control. The first thing I tell my clients is to stop using their credit cards. A person can't get out of debt while racking up higher credit card balances."

"As long as you pay the balance every month you'll be fine," Tristan countered.

"Fine until one month something happens and you can't pay the balance," she said. "Millions of people are struggling because they lost their jobs or had a pay cut or spent more than they bring in, and now find themselves under a mountain of debt. It's the worst feeling in the world, and if I can help someone escape from that living nightmare I will."

He studied her. "You're passionate about this."

"It's my job."

"Sounds more like a crusade."

"Possibly," she admitted. "After my parents divorced, my mom relied heavily on credit cards to survive. I can't help but think the stress of having so much debt and no way to pay it off contributed to her death."

Tristan reached across the table and touched Jayne's hand. "No wonder you feel the way you do."

She stared at his hand covering hers. His warmth comforted and soothed. "I'm sorry if I got carried away."

"No worries. I get it."

She jerked her gaze up to search his eyes. "Get what?"

"You," he said, as if they were talking about her favorite flavor of milkshake. "What you do is a calling, not just a job."

Alex, Molly and Serena knew that, but Rich had never really understood. Yet Tristan...

Jayne glanced down at his hand still covering hers.

He got it.

Got her.

That's what friends are for.

Surprise rippled through her, followed by an unfamiliar sense of contentment.

But he wasn't a friend. After tonight they would probably never see each other again, so his understanding her so well didn't matter. Truth was, he'd simply made a lucky guess.

Not so, her heart countered.

Jayne didn't listen. She couldn't.

She'd learned how dangerous, how risky, following her heart could be. It wasn't worth the gamble. She knew how easily feelings could lead you astray and affect your judgment.

She pulled her hand from under Tristan's, ignoring how cold she felt without the warmth of his touch.

The smart thing to do—the only thing she could do—was follow her head.

Jayne ignored the gorgeous pair of friendly green eyes staring down at her.

Better that way.

Safer that way.

Especially when a part of her wished the evening with Tristan didn't have to end. The best thing she could do was say goodbye to him. Forever.

CHAPTER FOUR

GRACE would be proud of him, Tristan thought as he drove Jayne home from the Mexican restaurant. The sparkle he remembered hadn't returned to her eyes, but they'd brightened more than once. Her lips had curved into a smile more easily as the day went on. And if she continued eating like she had tonight her weight loss would be a thing of the past and all her curves would return.

Yeah, Grace would be pleased.

Rich, not so much.

Tristan lifted a hand from the steering wheel to rub the sudden tension at the back of his neck.

His friend might have given him the okay to see Jayne and return the postcard, but he doubted Rich would be pleased with Tristan spending the afternoon and evening with her. Still, he had no regrets.

He'd liked getting to know Jayne the woman, not Jayne Rich's fiancée. She wasn't the typical kind of woman Tristan dated, but that made things more interesting.

He signaled, exited the freeway, and headed west from the off-ramp.

She was wary of him. Her eyes, body gestures and words made that clear. Tristan would have to show her he was more than Rich's best friend. But how?

Jayne yawned.

Tristan glanced her way. "Tired?"

"A little, but nothing a cup of coffee won't fix. Caffeine will wake me right up."

"Do you have plans tonight?" he asked, curious as to what she would do after he dropped her off.

"Not really plans," she admitted. "But I want to write my roommate ad."

She liked his idea. Tristan smiled. "Where do you plan on looking for a roommate?"

"I was thinking the internet—one of those networking sites, maybe?"

Uh-oh. The idea of her meeting strangers who responded to her ad didn't sound like such a good idea after all. "Be careful with the wording. You don't want to attract any crazies. Take a peek at the personals so you know what not to say."

"I'm looking for a roommate, not romance."

"A lot of those personal ads aren't interested in romance either."

"I appreciate the concern." She smiled at him. "I promise I'll be careful."

That didn't make him feel any better.

"The house is the third on the right," she said, in case he'd forgotten. He hadn't.

Tristan parked at the curve in front, set the emergency brake and turned off the ignition.

Her eyes widened. "You don't have to walk me to the door."

So much for her being careful. He pulled the keys out. "Yes, I do."

"But it's not a date."

"Walking someone to the door when it's dark outside is not only polite, it's also common sense," he cautioned. "You shouldn't take unnecessary risks."

"Oh—okay, then."

Tristan met her on the sidewalk. A light illuminated the front door of the bungalow. It was a nice little house with charming architectural details in a quiet neighborhood.

Hipsters, artsy types and surfers weren't going to want to live here. Maybe she could find a librarian to share the rent. Or a schoolteacher.

Maybe he was overreacting about this roommate search.

Jayne dug in her purse for her keys.

Not the safest action if she had been alone.

His concern over her safety rose.

What did a sheltered homebody know about scoping out roommates over the internet?

Probably nothing. That could lead to all kinds of trouble for her.

"So, what kind of roommate do you want?" he asked.

She climbed the first step of the porch. "Someone who is friendly, respectful, gainfully employed."

"What about sex?"

Her head swung toward him. "Sex?"

"Female or male."

"I…" She hesitated. "I've never lived with a guy, but I guess it would be okay as long as it was platonic. Of course it would depend on the person."

Open-minded. Good. But unsavory sorts still might apply. "Are there any other qualities you're looking for?"

"Why are you so interested in my future roommate?" she asked. "It's none of your business."

No, but Tristan didn't want someone taking advantage of her the way Rich had. "It could be."

"Come on," she said. "Getting a roommate might have been your idea, but it's not like you're applying for the position."

He hadn't been planning to do that at all, but if it kept her from taking in some predatory loser and gave him a reason to keep seeing her…

"I could."

No, he couldn't. Rich would kill him. Hell, Tristan would kill *himself*. Living with all that temptation sleeping in the next room and doing nothing about it.

But maybe he could play along, keep her considering him long enough to get to know him, see he wasn't Rich and weed out the really bad apples.

Then, when the right person presented herself, he could bow out. She would have her roommate, and he'd have gotten to enjoy her company and, by then, her kiss.

A perfect solution.

He hooked his thumb through a belt loop. "I know it might sound off the wall, considering how long we've known each other, but what would you think about me for a roommate?"

Tristan her new roommate?

Jayne stared up at him, baffled and unable to speak.

That wasn't an off-the-wall suggestion. It was total insanity.

She could think of a hundred better roommates, including Dr. Hannibal Lector or Norman Bates. Okay, a psychopathic killer might not be a better roommate, but at least she'd know where she stood with them.

With Tristan, she hadn't a clue. And the thought of seeing him every morning in the kitchen, or bumping into him in the hallway before bedtime, or imagining him in the shower...

Jayne balled her fingers around her keys until the metal edges dug into her skin.

Why was she even thinking about this? Jayne flexed her fingers.

"I don't think us being roommates would work," she said, not wanting to be rude or hurt his feelings.

"Why not?"

Darn him. He wasn't supposed to ask questions. All she wanted was for him to agree with her and say goodnight. Goodbye would be even better.

"Because..." She noticed the swarm of insects flying around the porch light. "You're Rich's best friend, and that would be too..."

Incestuous? Her cheeks warmed. No, that wasn't the right word.

"Awkward," she finally settled on. "Could you imagine what it would be like if you ever invited him over to the house?"

"I wouldn't. I'm hardly ever home, because of my job, and Rich has too much other stuff going on right now."

Like his wedding.

Jayne grimaced.

Tristan didn't seem to notice. "I wouldn't do anything to make you uncomfortable in your own home."

She appreciated his words, but his showing up today had done just that. Right now she was awfully uncomfortable. "That's my point. If you were paying rent it wouldn't be my home anymore. It would be…"

She couldn't bring herself to say *our home*.

Jayne continued. "I appreciate the offer…suggestion…but we don't know each other well enough to say we'd be compatible roommates."

"True, but you could say that about any potential roommate you'd find on the internet, too."

He had a point. Still…

"It's not a bad idea," he said. "I'm friendly, respectful and gainfully employed. I'm neat enough. And I have the single most important qualification you're looking for in a roommate."

Jayne had no idea what that might be. She couldn't imagine he'd have figured it out on his own after spending one day—half a day—with her. "What qualification is that?"

He smiled at her. "I love ice cream."

Reluctantly, she smiled back. Okay, she'd give him points for that one. But sharing a pint of Ben & Jerry's Chunky Monkey with him wouldn't be quite the same as it had with Molly.

"Just think about it," he said.

"I don't have to think about it," Jayne countered. "You'd probably eat all the ice cream."

"I know how to share, if that's what you're afraid of."

"I'm not afraid," she said, a little too quickly. "But a male roommate would be one more change. I've had enough of those in the last few months. Nothing personal, but it might be nice to have a roommate who would want to go with me to the nail salon."

Wicked laughter lit his eyes. "They do call it a *man*icure."

She glared at him.

He grinned. "You got me there. I've never stepped foot in a nail salon before. But there are a few advantages to having a male roommate you might not have considered."

Jayne should thank him for today and be done with it. With him. Except curiosity got the better of her. Again. "Such as?"

"Opening jars."

"I have a tool that can open anything."

"Changing lightbulbs."

He was going to have to come up with something a lot better than that. "I have a step ladder."

"Killing bugs."

She glanced up at the porch light, at the buzzing winged creatures. "Okay, you got me there."

"The one downside I see is my travel schedule," Tristan admitted. "I wouldn't be around much."

If he were her roommate his not being around would actually be a plus in his favor. Of course that would defeat one of her main purposes for getting a roommate as a cure for loneliness. "Yeah, I would rather live with someone who—"

"You weren't even considering a roommate until today," he interrupted. "Take some time to make an informed decision."

"You're right," she admitted. "But…"

"You're lonely," he said perceptively.

Her cheeks flushed.

"So let's use the time to get to know each other better," he suggested.

"I don't think—"

"How else will you know whether I'd be a good roommate or not?"

She was tempted. Appalled.

A mix of emotion churned inside her: relief at the thought of having someone to hang out with, and anxiety at realizing that the person was Rich's best friend. She had no idea about Tristan's motivation behind his roommate suggestion, but it didn't really matter. "I still know what my answer will be."

"You can always change your mind."

She'd had enough change in her life. She wasn't going to change for anyone—especially Tristan. "I won't."

A beat passed, then another.

"Then let me help you find a roommate," he offered. "I can be your guinea pig applicant."

"My guinea pig?"

"Yeah," he said. "You can learn my bad habits and figure out what your roommate deal-breakers are."

He was her ex-fiancé's best friend.

That was a pretty significant deal-breaker right there.

And yet...

Tristan had brought up a good point. She'd had roommates in college, and most recently Molly, but Jayne didn't know the first thing about what questions to ask. She'd entangled herself with the wrong fiancé. She didn't want to saddle herself with the wrong roommate.

And that could happen. Her judgment was obviously off. She didn't want to make another mistake, but she didn't know if trusting Tristan was the right move, either.

What you do is a calling, not just a job.

Yet he seemed to understand her and connect with her in a way only those closest to her had. But Alex, Molly and

Serena weren't here to help. Maybe Tristan's perception could help Jayne overcome her poor judgment and find the perfect roommate.

"Okay." She hoped this wasn't a mistake. "You can be my guinea pig as long as you're clear you won't be my roommate."

"I understand." A satisfied grin settled over Tristan's lips. "So I'll see you tomorrow night."

"Tomorrow?" she croaked.

He nodded. "You need practice getting to know me so you're ready when people answer your ad."

"I thought you said not to rush."

"This isn't rushing," he said. "It's preparation."

For what? she wondered. He seemed a little too slick and charming.

The porch light cast intriguing shadows on his handsome face. Jayne gazed up into Tristan's green eyes. Long, thick lashes like his really should be illegal on a man.

"I'll pick you up tomorrow night at seven."

"That sounds a lot like a date," she said.

"Not a date," Tristan countered. "We'll stay here and get to know each other."

"But what will we do?"

"Hang out."

She couldn't imagine her and Tristan sitting around and doing nothing. "We need something to do."

"You're the self-proclaimed homebody," he said. "What do you usually do?"

Jayne didn't want to confess to watching TV and organizing her socks or spice cabinet. "I…like to play Sudoku."

"We could play together."

He was easygoing, enthusiastic…and nearly impossible to resist. A lot like Rich when she'd met him. "I don't—"

"I should warn you, though, I'm going to win."

"I haven't even agreed to play with you yet."

"You have other plans?"

"I…" Of course not. "I'll have to check."

He pulled out a business card and handed it to her. "This has my cell number on it. Let me know if tomorrow works for you."

Tomorrow sounded so…soon. But the alternative was another night alone.

You're lonely, he'd said. Yes.

But not stupid.

She held the card tight between her fingers. "I'll think about it."

Inside the house, Jayne watched the taillights of Tristan's car grow smaller, until the two red dots disappeared down the street. She'd had fun today, but was happy he was gone. Maybe he'd decide he had better things to do than help her find a roommate.

She glimpsed Mrs. Whitcomb peeking through her lace curtains. Jayne smiled.

Nothing got past her neighbor. It had become more endearing than annoying. Especially once Molly had told Jayne how the woman had lost her husband of fifty-five years and all her children and grandchildren lived out of state. Most of the other neighbors felt the same way, and made sure to keep Mrs. Whitcomb in the know and even entertained.

Jayne placed the business card on the desk in the corner of the living room. She would decide later when—make that *if*—she wanted to see him again.

She noticed she had voicemail. Three messages, in fact. Only three people ever called. Well, sometimes four, when Cynthia, Molly's mom, dialed the number out of habit, but Jayne knew whose voices she'd hear on the other end.

Smiling, she picked up the phone and listened to the messages.

"Hi, it's Molly," a familiar voice said. "Sorry I missed your call. We were out looking at flooring, fixtures and furniture for the new house. Are you okay? I'm around. Call back."

"I got your message," Alex said. "Wyatt and I spent the day planning a much needed vacation to Tuscany. I'm home. I'll be up late. Call me."

"Hey, Jayne," Serena said. "I spoke with Molly and Alex. How are you doing? We want to have a chat tonight. Nine o'clock in the usual chatroom. It's time for us to catch up, so see you there."

Jayne glanced at the clock. Almost nine. She couldn't believe she'd spent that much time with Tristan. It hadn't seemed that long.

Without enough time to brew a cup of hot tea, she settled for a glass of iced tea instead. She skipped the cookies because she was full from dinner and all those tortilla chips.

She returned to the desk, sat, and logged into the chatroom. Too bad her webcam had broken or they could have done a video chat. Jayne wanted to see Molly now that she was seven months pregnant.

The chat window popped open on the monitor. Alex with her efficient blue font, Molly with her easy-to-read green font and Serena with her whimsical magenta font were chatting away.

Seeing their names and the words on the screen filled Jayne with warmth. Her three friends could see each other face-to-face any time in Las Vegas, but Jayne appreciated them taking the time so the four of them could still be together, albeit virtually.

Jayne: Hi.
Molly: You didn't sound like yourself on your message. Are you okay?
Alex: What's going on?
Serena: We're all yours tonight.

So many things were running through Jayne's head at the moment. Most of them having to do with Tristan, not Rich.

She wanted to tell her friends about yesterday, so typed everything that had happened at the teahouse, in order. Going there on her own. Seeing the Strickland sisters. Recognizing the woman—Deidre. Realizing Rich was getting married. Running away.

The words spilled out in a practical black font. It might have been the default font for the chat. Jayne didn't care. She knew her friends would offer an endless supply of support and love. The way they always had with each other.

But as she finished typing her experience at the teahouse, the hurt and betrayal she'd felt yesterday and this morning were all but gone. No sting remained. No tears welled in her eyes.

That pleased her.

"I'm not as bothered by it tonight," she wrote.

Jayne hit the "enter" key and stared at her blinking cursor.

Molly: Oh, Jayne. I'm happy you're feeling better, but I'm so sorry you had to go through that alone. How horrible.

Alex: I wish I had been there.

Molly: Me, too.

Serena: Me, three.

Alex: Jayne, I hate that you had to be hurt all over again. But Deidre's going to be the unhappy one in the end. Especially if she thinks that jerk will be faithful. Once a cheater, always a cheater.

Molly: That's for sure.

Serena: You're way too good for him.

Jayne: Thanks :) xoxox I'm over him, and he's the last person I'd ever want to be with, yet finding out he was getting married to her pretty much floored me.

Molly: You would have been shocked even if you two had had an amiable breakup. It hurt a lot more than I expected when I found out Doug was remarrying. And I was happy we'd divorced.

Alex: Is there anything you need, Jayne? Something we can do from here.

Jayne: You're doing it now. Thanks!

Molly: She's serious, Jayne.

Jayne: So am I.

Serena: Where were you when I called? I was worried when you didn't answer. I tried your cell, too.

Jayne: I was hiking at Torrey Pines. Or we might have been having dinner by then. I didn't hear my phone ring, sorry.

Alex: We?

Jayne: Me and Tristan.

Words flew across her monitor. Line after line of questions. Jayne had never known her friends could type so fast, and with such accurate spelling.

She laughed at the number of exclamation points and capital letters being used. And not just from Serena.

This was more entertaining than watching television. Jayne smiled.

The questions continued. One after another. No way could she answer them in real time, so she would wait until they'd finished. She sipped her tea as the words scrolled by.

Finally the typing stopped.

Serena: Hello, out there. We're waiting!!!!!

Jayne: Just wanted to make sure the three of you were finished with your questions first. Or maybe I should say inquisition.

Serena: :P

Molly: Spill. Now. Or face the consequences.

Alex: You won't like the consequences.

Jayne: LOL! But there's not much to tell.
Serena: We'll be the judges of that.
Jayne: His name is Tristan MacGregor. He's Rich's best friend and was going to be the best man at our wedding.
Alex: The photojournalist?
Jayne: Yes.
Molly: You said he was a hottie, if I remember correctly.
Jayne: I did?
Alex: You did.
Serena: Yes. I remember because you were hoping one of us might like him.
Molly: You thought having one of your bridesmaids fall in love with the best man would be romantic.
Jayne: I don't remember.
Alex: So tell us more about your date.
Jayne: It wasn't a date!

Anxiety rocketed through her, making each muscle tense. She didn't want to date Tristan. She didn't want to date period.

Jayne: Tristan just showed up on my doorstep because Rich's sister, Grace, was worried about me after yesterday at the teahouse.
Molly: So he shows up, the two of you go hiking, and then out to dinner?
Jayne: Yes. Well, we had iced tea and cookies here first.
Alex: That sounds like a date.
Jayne: We split the check.

She remembered how he'd wanted to pay until she reminded him they weren't on a date. Had she been wrong? No, he'd agreed it wasn't a date.

Serena: Did he kiss you goodnight?

Why would he kiss her? They hadn't been on a date.

But she'd been a tad disappointed he hadn't done…something. A handshake. A hug.

Jayne stiffened.

No, she hadn't been disappointed. She'd been relieved. Really, truly relieved. Rich's friend, his best man, remember?

Jayne: NO! No kiss!!!!
Molly: Are you going to see him again?
Jayne: He gave me his card and told me to call him so we could get together this week.
Serena: He wants to date you.
Alex: Definitely.
Jayne: He doesn't want to date me. He wants

A knock sounded at the door. Twice in one day? What was going on?

Serena: Wants what?
Jayne: Someone is at the door.
Molly: It's late. Ask who it is before you open the door.

"Who is it?" Jayne yelled.

"Tristan."

Every nerve-ending stood at attention. Her stomach did a cartwheel.

What was he doing back? She was about to stand up and find out when she remembered the chat. Her fingers flew across the keyboard.

Jayne: It's just Tristan. BRB

She rose from her chair and made her way to the front door. Curiosity clashed with apprehension. She unlocked and opened the door.

Tristan stood in her doorway the way he had earlier.

Okay, he was a hottie. Many women would agree. But Jayne wondered why she'd thought one of her friends might fit with him. Free-spirited, commitment-phobe Serena might have connected with Tristan on some level, but he wouldn't have been as good for her as steady and stable Jonas Benjamin.

"Hi," Tristan said, as if dropping by her apartment at this hour was normal.

"Hello." No doubt Mrs. Whitcomb would be happy she'd set her TiVo tonight. "Did you forget something?"

"No, but you did." He raised her boots and daypack in the air. "I thought you might need them if you caught the hiking bug today."

"Thanks." Jayne didn't want to be impressed, but she was. She took the items from him. "That was very thoughtful of you."

His mouth quirked. "We all have our moments."

She didn't trust him, but the guy had done her two favors today. Three if she counted his offer to help her with the roommate search. The least she could do was repay his kindness.

"If you're free Tuesday night, swing by after six," she said. "We can have a bite to eat, talk about my getting a roommate and see who is the Sudoku master."

His gaze held hers. "Sounds great."

She narrowed her eyes, ignoring the fluttering of her heart. "Just don't forget your wallet."

"Excuse me?"

She'd finally managed to surprise him. She grinned. "Loser buys the ice cream."

He laughed. "You're on."

Jayne stood at the doorway as he walked to his car. Once again she watched the taillights disappear down the street only this time knew exactly when she'd see him again. She sure hoped she hadn't made another mistake.

She returned to the desk and scanned her computer screen.

Serena: It's taking her a long time.
Alex: Too long. I hope she's okay.
Molly: If she's not back soon I'll call our neighbor, Mrs. Whitcomb. She's probably watching Jayne from her window now.
Alex: Unless they're inside.
Serena: I wonder if this is how my mother felt when I started dating?
Alex: If so, you owe her an apology.

Jayne frowned.
She was *not* dating. She was…
She typed. "Back! Sorry it took so long."

Alex: Is he gone?
Jayne: Yes, I forgot my hiking boots and daypack in his car so he was returning them.
Serena: That was nice of him.

He seemed nice. Very nice, in fact. But appearances could be deceiving.

Jayne: So, where were we?
Molly: You said Tristan didn't want to date you, but you never told us what he does want.

Jayne didn't want her friends' pity because Tristan didn't want to date her. The truth was he did want to spend time with her, and that made her feel good—even if he was Rich's best friend.

Jayne: Tristan just wants to move in with me. But don't worry. I said no.

CHAPTER FIVE

MONDAY dragged. Tuesday, too.

Tristan had a story due, but seeing Jayne was the only thing on his mind. A phone conversation with Grace had appeased her concerns, but talking about the lovely Jayne and thinking about they day they'd spent together only added to his impatience.

When their date on Tuesday finally arrived, he sat across from her at the patio table in her backyard. She looked hot in her lime-green T-shirt. The stretchy fabric accentuated her breasts. A great view, but if he didn't stop admiring her he would lose. Again.

Tristan focused on his Sudoku puzzle. Numbers from one to nine filled many of the boxes. Only a few more to go. Jayne was smart and fast, but he would not lose this time.

"Finished," she said.

No way. He glanced at his watch. Six and a half minutes. He set his pen on the table. "You *are* the Sudoku Master."

She bit her lip. "Do you want to play again?"

"You won three out five games."

"We can make it even," she suggested.

"Or you could beat me again," he countered.

"But I wouldn't."

"What do you mean?"

She stared down at her puzzle.

"You would *let* me win?" he guessed, unable to keep the disbelief from his voice.

A charming pink colored her cheeks. "It's just a game."

"Exactly."

"Well, sometimes it's easier if the other person doesn't like to lose."

"You mean Rich."

Her cheeks turned even redder. "He liked winning."

"So do I. But I can still be a good sport if I lose."

The doubt in Jayne's eyes told Tristan she didn't believe him. No matter what he said or did, when she looked at him she must see Rich. Changing that opinion might take time. Time he really didn't have with a new assignment coming up.

The setting sun provided the perfect backdrop to her dark shiny hair. A golden aura, almost like a halo, surrounded her. She reminded him of an angel—one who needed to learn to use her wings. He might not have the time, but he wasn't ready to give up on her yet.

"I'm sorry," she muttered.

"You don't have to apologize for being good at something, especially after that amazing dinner."

"I made the lasagna. The bread came from the bakery and the salad from the garden." She narrowed her eyes, but couldn't keep the corners of her mouth from curving upward. "But if you think flattery will get you out of buying the ice cream tonight, think again."

He grinned, more at ease than he could remember being in a long time. Maybe being her roommate wasn't such a crazy idea.

What was he? Nuts? Even if she had a change of heart, he could never live with her. The separate bedrooms clause was a total deal-breaker for him. "Hey, a guy's gotta try."

That was his problem. Even though he knew Jayne was his best friend's ex-fiancée, he couldn't stop himself from wanting to be with her himself.

She laughed.

The warm sound flowed through him, as if his blood were as thick as honey, and filled up all sorts of empty places he hadn't known he had. Tristan had never felt anything like it, and he wasn't sure he liked the feeling. He shifted in his seat. "Seriously, though, I'm only giving compliments where they're due."

She blushed again. "Thank you."

"You're welcome."

With her pink-tinged cheeks and bright blue eyes she was more than another pretty face. Not many people put other's feelings before their own the way Jayne did. Her sharp intellect kept him intrigued and entertained. And her honesty made him feel he could trust her even though they were still getting to know each other.

Rich had really screwed up letting Jayne get away.

His loss, Tristan's gain?

Except he was looking for fun, a good time, not something serious. His job didn't allow for that. Even if it did, he wasn't looking to make a commitment. Now or in the future.

A dog yipped. The high-pitched sound made him think of the small, ankle-biter type.

"Quiet, Duke," Jayne called to the fence.

The barking stopped.

"Sorry," she said. "I usually take him for a walk after dinner. We're starting a dog agility class on Thursday, so we've been practicing a little, too."

He glanced toward the spot where the sound came from. Across the freshly mowed grass, next to the fence, was a small garden. "Is that where you got the salad from?"

She nodded. "I've been trying to make sure Molly's hard work doesn't go to waste. She used to spend so much time working out here."

Little signs marked each of the neat, straight rows of what he assumed were vegetables. He didn't know anything about gardening himself, but he liked eating what came from them. "So how's it going?"

"Well, I did some yardwork when I was a kid, but never gardening, so I've been learning as I dig in the dirt, plant and prune. There's been a bit of trial and error," Jayne admitted, "but I haven't killed anything yet. Molly will be happy when she sees it."

"What about you? Does working in the garden make you happy, Jayne?"

Looking at the garden, she crinkled her nose until a satisfied smile settled on her lips. "Actually, I'm enjoying myself more than I thought I would."

"I'm not surprised."

"Why do you say that?"

"It's all about putting down roots," he said. "That's what you want, and you're good at it."

Girlfriend material, sure. Wife material, most definitely.

Tristan didn't want either. So what in the hell was he doing here?

He picked up his glass of lemonade and drank. The tart sweetness matched his mood.

Jayne didn't need a roommate. She needed a husband. Best to cut his losses and say goodbye.

"You know, I never thought about it like that," she said.

Her features looked more animated. Too bad he didn't have his camera out here. Though he probably had enough pictures of her to last a lifetime.

She continued. "I think you're right."

He'd bet a million dollars he was correct. He wished he were wrong.

She sipped her lemonade. He did the same, listening to the sounds of the neighborhood. A child's squeal could be heard over a lawnmower. A woman called her family inside for dinner.

The noises were more foreign to him than gunfire, thanks to his being embedded with a unit in Afghanistan. He'd avoided this kind of life in the suburbs before. The life his ex-wife wanted. The life Jayne wanted.

I hope that happens someday.

Someday, she'd said. Not now.

Maybe he didn't have to bolt out of here. She'd told him she wasn't looking for a relationship at the moment. That could mean she would be up for something more…casual.

She set her glass on the table. "Do you garden?"

He rarely noticed landscaping unless it caught his eye for a possible photograph or food. "Digging in dirt doesn't appeal to me."

"Do you live in an apartment?"

"Hotel."

Her mouth formed an o. "A hotel?"

Tristan thought of the mega-story steel and glass building—one of San Diego's most luxurious hotels—he currently called home. At least until his next assignment came up. "Yes."

"Why?"

"Staying at hotels is easier than renting an apartment," he said. "It gives me the flexibility I need with my travel schedule. Plus I can always move if I don't like it or get bored."

"So you don't even want to commit to a six month lease?"

"I don't like leaving a place empty for so long."

"What about your stuff?" she asked.

"Stuff?" he asked.

"Books, CDs, computer, clothing, old report cards. You know…stuff," she explained. "When I moved from my apartment into here I had so many boxes. Mementoes from when I was a kid. Things I never want to let go of."

"Everything I own fits into a couple of plastic bins, so it's easy to move from place to place."

"I could never fit all my kitchen stuff in a couple of bins." She sounded grateful for that. "I grew up moving around a lot. 'Live light, move light,' my father used to say. But a person needs to have some things that have meaning or hold memories for them."

"I have those things," Tristan said. "It just all fits into the bins."

"So living out of a suitcase really works for you?"

"Yes."

"But how do you know if you're traveling or not?" she asked. "You're never home if you live in a hotel."

"The hotel is my home."

"So you always go back to the same hotel? The same room?"

"Well, no…" Her reaction didn't surprise him, but it did make him vaguely defensive. "My life makes sense for me. I travel too much to take care of a place. I'd just be wasting money paying for an empty apartment. This way I check in and out as need be."

"If you had a roommate, your place wouldn't be empty."

He raised a brow. "Are you offering?"

"Just offering up the great suggestion you gave me," she said. "Living at a hotel has to be really expensive."

"I can afford it."

"If you can afford the nightly rate at a hotel, then you can afford to buy a place."

His ex-wife, Emma, had wanted to buy a house and have a baby before their first anniversary. Finally an adult and free from college at twenty-two, Tristan had wanted her to travel with him around the world while he took photographs. Hell, at *thirty*-two that still sounded like a good way to spend a year or two. "I'm not looking to make a thirty-year commitment to a mortgage anytime in the near future."

"I'd hope not." Jayne sounded aghast. "That would be a huge mistake."

That didn't sound like the domestically inclined, angelic homebody he'd come to know tonight. Intrigued, Tristan leaned toward her. "I'm surprised you agree with me."

"Of course I agree with you. Who wouldn't?" Lines creased her forehead, the way they did anytime she got serious about something. "You should never take out a thirty-year mortgage. Fifteen-year mortgages are the only ones that make financial sense these days."

Tristan would have laughed except for the sincerity in her voice. The last thing he wanted to do was hurt her feelings when she was trying to be helpful.

Surprisingly, he found this financially astute side of her utterly charming and totally appealing. He respected her dedication to her job and what she believed even, if it were the exact opposite of his thinking. "I'll have to remember that if I ever buy a house."

"Not if, when," she said. "Seriously, Tristan, buying a condo or a townhouse and finding a roommate would be such a smart move right now with the current market conditions. You'll build equity fast as the market rises again rather than throw your dollars away living at a hotel."

She sure was tenacious when it came to money. He leaned back in his chair. "Home ownership just isn't for me."

"There are tax benefits." She said the words as if she were dangling a cookie in front of him.

"Why aren't *you* taking advantage of the tax benefits?" he asked.

"Excuse me?"

"You rent," he pointed out.

"Well, yes. I like living in Molly's bungalow," Jayne said. "But I can't wait to buy a house of my own."

He thought about the house he'd grown up in, on the same street where Rich's parents still lived, and the bigger one his parents lived in now. "Saving up for a big, splashy house with an ocean view?"

"No, a fixer-upper would be best." Her eyes sparkled. "For as long as I can remember, through all the countries and different bases where I lived as a kid, I've dreamed about owning my own house. Putting down roots, as you said."

The passion in her voice appealed to him on a gut level. Tristan didn't want a house for himself, but he wanted Jayne to have one. "What's stopping you?"

"There are a few things I need to do first."

"Like what?"

"I need to save enough for a down payment and get married."

Tristan did a double take. The down payment he understood. The marriage part, not so much.

He thought Jayne might be joking, but one look at the determined set of her jaw told him she wasn't. Still, he needed to state the obvious. "You don't have to be married to buy a house."

"I know, but it just seems…I guess it seems like the easiest way."

"Easier if you need two salaries to qualify for a mortgage," he conceded. "But marital status shouldn't stop anyone from buying a house. Lots of single women and men buy houses. Look at your friend who owns this place. She's single. Or was single."

"Molly and her ex-husband purchased this house when they were married. She bought Doug out when they divorced."

"Bad example. But there are lots of other good ones out there," Tristan said. "Maybe in our parents' generation women waited. But you shouldn't wait to buy a house if that's what you want to do."

"I'm not really that old-fashioned." She sounded defensive. "But I guess I've always imagined things happening in a certain order in my life. Marriage comes before a house."

"So this thing with Rich really messed with your plans, huh?"

She swallowed. Nodded.

Just because things with Rich didn't work out doesn't mean I can't live happily ever after here in San Diego with my one true love.

Tristan felt like a real heel.

He wasn't a big fan of plans. Emma had been full of them. But at least sweet Jayne was up-front about hers. She wasn't hiding who she was or what she wanted. Or demanding he change what he was and what he wanted.

"Imagine and plan all you want," he said. "But if you dream of owning a house you should go for it. Now, if you're able."

"That would be like asking me to jump out of a fully operational airplane. I couldn't do it."

"Jumping out of an airplane isn't so scary," Tristan said. "It gets easier each time."

"How many times have you jumped out of an airplane?"

He shrugged. "More than fifty. Less than a hundred."

Her eyes widened. "That's…insane."

"Insane fun," he agreed. "I'll have to show you the photographs."

Her mouth dropped. "You take your camera with you?"

"Never leave home without it."

"And I just never leave home." She laughed. "We're quite the odd couple."

"Not so odd."

"And not a couple."

Too bad.

Although…

Maybe they did want different things in the long term. That didn't mean a short-term relationship couldn't work between them.

He could help her loosen up and have fun. He could show her she could pursue her dream of putting down roots without a husband by her side.

Jayne could help him, too. She had brought up a good point. Maybe it was time he stopped living out of a suitcase. Some mornings he'd wake up and forget where he was.

Not to mention if Jayne got what she wanted—her own house—maybe he could get what he wanted—her.

"I have an idea," he said.

"Not roommates again."

"No, houses."

She straightened.

Good, he had her attention. "Maybe I was a little quick to shoot down the idea of buying a place. If the market's that good—"

"It is."

"I suppose I could see what's out there," he conceded. "Having a home base might make sense, and it sounds like it could be a better move financially."

"A much better move."

"I'd need someone to look with me." He would make sure they looked at condominiums for him and houses for Jayne. "You interested?"

"I love looking at real estate, but I'm not the right person to do this with you."

"I trust your judgment."

"You shouldn't," she said, without any hesitation. "We're looking for completely different things."

He could see her point, but still…"Are you sure I can't change your mind?"

"No." The determined set of her jaw told him she meant it. "I'm sure you can find someone else to go with you."

"Sure, but I know at least you'd be honest with."

"That's the problem, Tristan," she admitted. "You wouldn't like what I had to say."

Thursday night, Jayne slipped out of her shoes. Her feet ached. She'd had a long day at work, followed by a dog agility class with Mrs. Whitcomb's Duke.

Ice cream sounded really good. Jayne thought about Tuesday night and the ice cream cone Tristan had purchased for her…with his credit card. She shook her head.

Tristan MacGregor needed help. The guy used his credit card for everything and lived in a hotel. He'd deluded himself into living a life based on credit and borrowing, but she wasn't the one to help him. They'd said goodnight. She'd considered it goodbye.

Jayne padded her way into the kitchen. Before she reached the freezer, the telephone rang.

Alex, Molly or Serena?

Smiling, Jayne picked up the telephone receiver from the charger on the counter. "So, what was the high temperature in Vegas today?"

"I have no idea," Tristan said. "But if you give me a minute I can check *weather.com*."

"Tristan. I'm so sorry. I thought you were one of my friends." Jayne cringed, realizing how that must have sounded. Like she didn't have many friends. Like she didn't think of him as a friend. "Other friends, I mean."

Shut up, Jayne.

Mercifully, he changed the subject. "How was the class with your neighbor's dog tonight?"

She couldn't believe he'd remembered. "We both got a workout and met some nice people."

"Good." He paused. "And the roommate search? I never asked. Have you posted an ad yet?"

"No." She leaned against the counter, realizing how empty the house suddenly felt. Eating a bowl of ice cream alone was no longer so appealing. "My friends wanted to look over my ad first."

"Good friends."

"The best." Thinking about Alex, Molly and Serena brought another smile to Jayne's face. "I realized it would be nice to have someone living here, but there's no real hurry. I want to make sure I do this roommate thing right and not rush into anything."

"Smart thinking," he said. "Never rush into making any big decisions."

She tightened her fingers around the receiver. "I learned that lesson the hard way."

"With Rich."

Jayne swallowed. "Yes."

"Tough," Tristan said sympathetically.

"You have no idea," she said, a trace of bitterness creeping into her voice.

"Actually, I do." His words surprised her. Could he actually be trying to alleviate her discomfort?

"Your ex-wife?" she guessed.

Silence filled the line. It must be his turn to feel uncomfortable.

"Yeah," he said finally.

She thought about her own experience. "Because you got engaged too soon?"

"Because we got engaged at all," he said frankly. "I met Emma during freshman orientation in college. By senior year everyone, including both our families, expected us to get married. It was what she wanted. So I proposed."

"Is that what you wanted?" Jayne asked.

"It was what I thought I was supposed to want. So we had a big wedding after we graduated."

"You were young."

"Too young," he admitted. "I didn't think I'd rushed into the decision at the time, but college is its own bubble world. If I'd just put a little more thought into it I would have waited until after graduation and we were supporting ourselves to propose. Turns out Emma didn't like being the wife of a struggling photojournalist. She wanted me to go work for my father instead."

"Didn't she know that you wanted to be a photographer?"

"We talked about it, sure, but I guess not nearly enough. She thought I'd change my mind. I tried."

"Changing your mind?"

"Being a desk jockey. I hated it. Even my dad said I wasn't cut out for the office and told me to give photojournalism a shot."

"You could have tried counseling."

"We did," he said, surprising Jayne yet again. "I just couldn't make myself into the man she wanted me to be. She didn't want the kind of life my job required. We gave it two years, but after we'd exhausted every other option divorce seemed to be the only alternative."

She appreciated Tristan opening up the way he had. Most guys she knew wouldn't have.

"When my father finally wanted out of marriage he just left," she confided. "No compromising. No counseling. Nothing. At least you tried to save your marriage. That says a lot."

Maybe Tristan MacGregor wasn't an identical cookie cutter image of Rich after all.

"Tried, but didn't succeed. Emma found what she was looking for. She married a doctor, lives in Laguna Beach and has kids now."

"What about you?" Jayne asked. "Have you found what you wanted?"

"I have everything I want." Tristan said. "But getting to this point hurt someone I loved. I never want that to happen again."

"I wish learning the big lessons didn't have to hurt so much."

"If they didn't hurt, we wouldn't learn."

"Good point," she said.

He cleared his throat. "Speaking of learning, I'm planning to look at condominiums on Sunday. I'd still like you to go with me. I know I could learn a lot from you."

Jayne nearly dropped the phone.

Say no. That was all she had to do. They were looking for different things in homes and from life. Yet she felt closer to Tristan after the conversation they'd just shared.

He was still Rich's best friend.

But Tristan wasn't exactly like Rich or…her father. Oh, Tristan still had problems. He knew nothing about finances. He lived in the now without regard to tomorrow. And he couldn't even commit to a six-month lease let alone a relationship.

But, like her, he'd made mistakes and learned hard lessons. She didn't want that to happen to him with his real estate search.

She could help him.

She wanted to help him.

"I might have some free time on Sunday," Jayne said.

Of course she had the time.

But did she have the courage?

CHAPTER SIX

LOOKING at condominiums with Jayne was more fun than Tristan had thought it would be. He was happy she'd decided to change her mind and come with him today. He tapped his thumb against the steering wheel to the uplifting beat of the song on the radio.

Maybe by the time they were finished with their open house tour he could change her mind about a few other things, too.

As he flicked on his blinker to move to the right lane of the freeway, he glanced toward the passenger seat. Jayne sat with a three-inch binder full of real estate information on her lap.

Leave it to Jayne to come so prepared.

He'd brought the real estate section from the paper, but he had no plan of attack. His best shots were often as much a result of luck as of planning, so he was comfortable winging it.

Tristan should have known Jayne would think otherwise. She'd charted their entire day, printing out directions, maps and information on each listing.

Organized and orderly.

Not such a bad thing, Tristan realized.

He and Jayne might be different in the way they approached things, but they had more in common than he'd realized. Similar tastes in architecture and interiors and food. They made a good team. A very good team.

Now all he had to do was convince her to play with him. Maybe after their next stop. He smiled.

"What's so funny?" she asked.

"Just thinking about the day so far." And how he would like it to end with a little one-on-one contact.

"We've seen so much." Excitement laced her words.

He wondered whether she was excited about the real estate or him.

"I really can see you living in the beachfront condo," she added.

Real estate. Damn. But he wasn't giving up.

"So can I." Her observation didn't surprise him. They were getting to know each other better every time they walked through a property. "The location is perfect. I really like the layout of the place."

She nodded. "Don't forget the kitchen. It's to die for."

"It is nice as far as kitchens go," Tristan admitted. "But, face it, any kitchen would be an improvement over what I have now."

"You don't have a kitchen."

"Exactly," he said. "But I do get nightly turndown service and a chocolate on my pillow."

Jayne dimpled. "True, but think of all the chocolate you can store in those gorgeous maple cupboards. One piece versus many pieces. Seems a no-brainer to me."

Tristan slowed to allow a truck to merge onto the freeway. "You may be right."

He exited the freeway.

"Wait a minute," she said with surprise. "Where are we going?"

A smug smile settled on his lips. She was going to love this. "It's a surprise."

She leaned back against the seat. "I don't like surprises."

Her tone and reaction bothered him.

No, Tristan assured himself, Jayne needed this whether she thought so or not.

He stopped at the red light at the bottom of the ramp. "Why don't you like surprises?"

Her full lips pressed together.

"Come on," he urged.

She shook her head.

He turned west when the light changed to green. "Talk to me, Jayne."

She stared straight ahead out the windshield, her expression carefully blank. "Three days before our wedding Rich sent me a text saying he had a surprise waiting for me at his apartment. Only I'm guessing he must have sent the message to me by mistake. When I got to his apartment—"

"Okay." Tristan gripped the steering wheel until his knuckles turned white. "I get the picture."

"So did I," she said bitterly. "He was with Deidre when I arrived."

Tristan knew that. Oh, man, he knew. He'd just never faced the emotional impact it must have had on Jayne. His insides twisted. "Jayne—"

"Sorry," she said quickly. "I shouldn't have told you."

"That's okay." But it wasn't. A lump of guilt the size of a basketball lodged in his throat. "I asked."

He wished he hadn't.

Because Rich hadn't sent the text message to Jayne. Tristan had…

Tristan stood in the dressing area of the tuxedo rental shop. He'd already tried on his tux while waiting for Rich, who was running late.

Rich strutted out of his dressing room wearing a black tux. "This will work."

"Not bad," Tristan said.

"Jayne will like it."

Tristan nodded. Jayne would love it. "So, you must be breathing easier with Deidre out of the way."

Rich stared at his reflection in a three-panel mirror. He smoothed the lapels, turned and checked out his backside. "I haven't broken up with her."

Tristan's mouth gaped. "You're getting married this weekend."

Rich shrugged. "She's coming over to my apartment tonight."

"Cutting it a little close, bud."

"I'm not breaking up with Deidre," he said. "I'm in love with her."

Tristan couldn't believe what he was hearing. Rich had never acted like this before. "What about Jayne?"

"Jayne thinks I'm working a shift for someone tonight so I can have more time off for the wedding and honeymoon. She'll never know."

"You idiot." Tristan's temper flared. "You can't promise to love her, to cherish her, when you're seeing another woman."

Rich turned red. "I promised to marry her. I'm keeping my promise. It's the only honorable thing to do."

"You're cheating on her." Tristan lowered his voice so no one in the other part of the shop would hear them. "That's not honorable."

"So you'd rather I broke Jayne's heart?" Rich shook his head. "I'm a man of my word. I'm the only one she's got. Maybe once the wedding's over things will get better."

"What about Deidre?"

"Things are already great with her," Rich said.

The guy didn't have a clue, but Tristan would be shirking his best man and best friend duty if he didn't say something. "You're the closet thing I have to a brother, but I have to tell you, dude, you're screwing up big-time. Forget Jayne. Forget Deidre. You're not ready to get married."

Rich's nostrils flared. "Says the divorced guy?"

A beat passed. And another.

This wasn't a game of one-on-one or one-upmanship. This was real life. Rich's life.

"Yeah, I'm divorced." Tristan rocked back on his heels. "And you of all people should remember what that was like for me. Hell on earth. My worst nightmare. I don't want you to experience that, but if you marry Jayne this weekend you will. I guarantee it."

"Hey, I know you mean well, but Jayne's parents were divorced. It was messy and really affected her," Rich said. "She won't divorce me."

Tristan stared at his buddy in disbelief. "So you'll spend the rest of your life being married and miserable?"

Rich stuck out his jaw—a sure sign he wasn't going to listen to reason. "I'll be fine."

What about Jayne? Tristan didn't think she'd be fine. "You have to tell her."

"I don't have to do anything except show up at the church on Saturday."

"Maybe if you talked to her—"

"I'm not talking. And you better not say anything, either."

"Rich—"

His best friend's gaze held his. "You promised me."

"Dude—"

"You always said you had my back," Rich reminded him. "You can't let me down now."

Tristan swore savagely.

Rich smiled in satisfaction, recognizing his capitulation. "These shoes are a little tight. I'm going to see if they have a larger size."

He walked out of the dressing room area and into the main shop.

Unbelievable. Tristan dragged his hand through his hair. Rich needed to listen to him and call the wedding off.

A cellphone rang. The sound came from Rich's dressing room.

Tristan glanced inside. A cellphone sat on top of a pair of board shorts.

You always said you had my back.

Maybe if he had more time he could talk some sense into Rich, but with only three days until the wedding…Tristan couldn't let Rich ruin his life and Jayne's, too.

Promise me you won't.

Tristan couldn't say anything. But maybe he could *do* something.

He looked again at the cellphone. Jayne was calling.

Maybe it was a sign.

Maybe…

Damn, he didn't have much time. Rich could return any minute.

Tristan urgently typed a text message: *Be @ my apt 8 pm for big surprise.*

This was for Rich's own good, Tristan told himself. For his future happiness. And Jayne's, too.

Not wanting to waste another second, he hit "send."

Seven months later, Tristan still believed he'd done the right thing to keep both Rich and Jayne from making the mistake of their lives. But maybe he could have accomplished the same thing in a less cruel way.

He'd hurt Jayne. More than he realized.

Tristan took a left hand turn.

Maybe he could make it up to her.

He'd been less than honest then. He couldn't be less than honest now. "About that surprise—"

"I don't know why I brought it up now." She looked at him with regret.

His stomach clenched. He had to tell her the truth. "There's something—"

"Stop. Please." Her gaze implored his. "What happened with Rich is in the past. That's where I want to leave it. I only want to look forward now. Okay?"

Tristan wanted to tell her the truth, but he also wanted to do what she asked. He sure as hell didn't want to cause her any more pain. The truth would hurt her. He had no doubt about that.

He weighed his options.

Jayne had admitted she was relieved she hadn't married Rich. Maybe how she'd found out the truth about the cheating wasn't that big a deal. Not telling her sure would make things easier for Tristan.

"Okay," he agreed.

She gazed out the passenger window. "This is such a cute neighborhood."

He appreciated her comment—a distraction to bridge the awkwardness. "Yes."

Bungalows and cottages lined the street. A twentysomething woman pushed a baby stroller on the sidewalk while a chocolate Lab trotted next to her. "It's a great location—walking distance to shops and the library."

At least that was what the listing agent had told him when he'd called her yesterday for more information.

"But I don't see any condominiums or townhouses," Jayne said.

He parked in front of an open house sign.

She gasped.

The cottage with a "For Sale" stuck in the overgrown front yard defined the term fixer-upper. The white picket fence had seen better days. The exterior needed paint. The porch railing was splintered and broken.

Uh-oh, Tristan thought. Maybe this hadn't been such a good idea.

Except the price was right, and Jayne was staring at the little house as if it were a big, beautiful castle straight from the pages of a fairytale.

"I don't understand." Her gaze remained fixed on the house. "You want don't want to buy a house."

"No," he admitted. "But you do."

She turned to look at him. With her eyes wide and her nose crinkled she looked oh-so-adorable. "Me?"

All his doubts vanished in that instant. He'd made the right choice bringing her here.

"We're here to look at a house for you, Jayne." Tristan grinned. "Not me."

Standing in the dream-come-true cottage, Jayne ran her fingers along the built-in buffet in the dining room. She would never have expected Tristan MacGregor to take something she associated as bad—a surprise—and turn it into something so good.

"What do you think?" he asked.

"A fresh coat of paint would spruce this right up." Jayne wondered what kind of wood lay underneath the chipped and battered green paint. Going natural might work, too.

"You like the house?"

"Yes." She spoke calmly, considering inside she felt like a kid on a shopping spree in a toy store. She loved everything she'd seen so far, and even knew where the Christmas tree should go, but something kept her from showing her excitement. "The house has lots of potential."

Someone, she realized, not something.

Jayne couldn't fathom how Tristan, of all people, had found this nice little neighborhood in a great location and this quaint fixer-upper—a house that was everything she could have ever hoped to own. It was if he'd peeked inside her heart somehow and turned what he'd seen into reality.

That bothered her. Okay, scared her.

Because Jayne didn't know whether to hit him or hug him.

"Check in here," he said.

She peeked around the corner. "A clawfoot tub."

"Look at the hand-held shower head." He pointed to the tub. "That could make showering interesting."

The last thing Jayne wanted to think about was Tristan in the shower. She glanced around the bathroom. "If I took out the vanity and put in a pedestal sink there would be room for a stall shower."

"That would be a lot of work and expense."

Jayne shrugged. "Not that much, considering everything else that needs to be fixed is cosmetic. Paint, flooring, some trim."

"The house seems priced right."

She nodded.

"So you could afford it."

It wasn't a question. "I…"

She could afford the foreclosed, bank-owned property on her own. No husband required to purchase the charming house.

Imagine and plan all you want. But if you dream of owning a house you should go for it. Now, if you're able.

Her heart bumped. She felt a flutter in her stomach.

But she couldn't. Not really.

Still, the possibility, the temptation, left her conflicted and confused.

Jayne liked everything to go according to plan. She resented Tristan for creating uncertainty. She didn't want—didn't need—that right now.

"I could afford it if I wanted to buy a house on my own. Which I don't," she said. For his sake or hers, she wasn't certain.

"But you could," he stressed.

She wished he would be quiet.

A young married couple glanced into the bathroom and continued to the bedrooms. The pair held hands as they walked, reminding her of everything she'd dreamed of having.

Jayne's chest tightened. "You don't get it. I wanted… I want to be like them."

"Who?" Tristan asked.

"That couple," she whispered. "I want to look and pick out a house with my husband."

"Just see the possibilities, Jayne."

His smile sent an unwelcome burst of heat rushing through her veins. She gritted her teeth.

The platinum blonde realtor hosting the open house ran after the young couple like a hawk looking for prey.

"What possibilities?" Jayne asked.

"Whatever ones you can imagine," he said. "Just because we're looking at a house and you like one doesn't mean I expect you to buy it."

"I know that."

Except she wanted to buy it.

Jayne bit her lip. No, she didn't.

"Lighten up," he encouraged. "You don't always have to be so serious about everything."

She raised her chin. "Says the man who can't commit to an apartment lease."

He laughed.

"Anyway, I'm not always that serious," she added.

He eyed the thick, heavy binder she held.

"You wanted help," Jayne said, in her defense. "I like being prepared, but that doesn't mean I'm not trying to have fun."

"Stop trying." His tone softened. "Let the fun happen."

His words sank in, like rain against dry soil after a long, hot summer.

Hadn't she been telling herself the same thing about relationships? Love would find her when she wasn't looking. The same way it had found Alex, Molly and Serena.

Jayne wet her dry lips.

"I'll help you," he offered.

She eyed him warily. "How?"

"Having fun is my specialty," he said. "You're young, Jayne."

"I'm twenty-eight."

"Young," he reiterated. "I know you want that happily-ever-after, but even you said not now. Someday."

She nodded.

"So stop being so serious and have fun. Explore, look at houses you might want to own, experience, date."

The air whooshed from her lungs. She struggled for a breath. "I'm really not looking—"

"For a relationship," he finished. "Casual dating is different. What's holding you back?"

Nothing. Except Jayne wasn't an explorer. She didn't like new experiences and she'd never casually dated in her life. "I..."

But what she'd done in the past hadn't worked.

She stepped out into the hallway and looked around. Finding this place had shown her what was possible. Not today or tomorrow, but someday.

Maybe if she adopted a more casual attitude toward dating and embraced fun the way Tristan did she would finally find what her friends had found in Las Vegas. She would find love.

Or rather, love would find her.

She straightened. "Nothing is holding me back."

Tristan smiled at her. "Then let me show you how."

Anticipation flew through her like a boomerang. "But you're Rich's—"

"Casual and fun, Jayne," Tristan countered. "Emphasis on the fun."

Fun? With Rich's best man?

With Rich's best friend?

With a man who didn't believe in marriage or happy endings?

That would make him...

Perfect, she realized.

Tristan was actually the perfect person to show her how to have fun. Even date casually. He was the last person she would ever fall for—the last man she could ever have a future with. Her heart would be safe, reserved for the real thing when it found her.

"Casual and fun," she repeated.

"What do you say?" he asked.

Jayne grinned. "Sounds good to me."

CHAPTER SEVEN

TONIGHT was the night. Tristan glanced at Jayne, sitting beside him in the front seat.

This first date would give her a glimpse of the good times ahead. One taste and she would embrace the concept of casual and fun. Embrace him, too.

He'd never had to work this hard for a woman. He was no believer in delayed gratification. But Jayne, with her bright eyes and caring heart and sexy body, was worth the wait and the effort.

Everything tonight would be perfect. He'd made sure by taking a page out of Jayne's playbook and planning ahead. He couldn't wait to see her reaction.

Tristan parked his car at the Loews Coronado Bay Resort, grabbed his camera bag from the back seat and made his way around to the passenger side. He opened Jayne's door. "Don't forget your jacket."

She tossed her jacket over her left forearm and slid out of the car. "I just love Coronado. I lived here when I was six."

Her wide smile that reached all the way to her baby blues hit him right in the solar plexus. He nearly stumbled back. Somehow he managed to close the car door.

He'd wanted her to be pleased with tonight, but his reaction to her caught him off-guard. Then again, an attractive woman could take any man by surprise. He cleared his throat. "You'll have to show me around."

Her eyes gleamed with excitement. "Tonight?"

Seeing her so happy filled him with warmth. Jayne needed this. She needed him.

"Another time." He swung the strap of his camera pack over his shoulder. "I have plans for tonight."

"Plans?" Jayne's nose crinkled. "I thought fun was just supposed to happen."

"Fun can be spontaneous," he explained. "But extra-special fun takes a little planning."

Her mouth quirked. "Extra-special fun, huh?"

"You'll see."

Tristan placed one hand at the small of her back. The palm of his hand fit nicely, comfortably, against her. He led her inside the resort hotel.

A group of men and women in track outfits and with camera cases stood at the front desk. Two men in tuxedos spoke with the concierge. Uniformed bellhops rolled luggage carts.

"Have you been here before?" he asked.

Jayne looked around. "No, this place was a little out of our budget back then. It probably still is."

A grand split staircase with brass railings stood out in the lobby. Chandeliers added an air of elegance. Large windows provided ocean views. But Jayne was the only thing he wanted to look at.

"It's absolutely lovely." She eyed him mischievously. "I think I might like having extra-special fun with you."

Tristan knew without a doubt he'd enjoy it. The thought of the evening ending with more than a goodnight kiss was looking better and better. "You might even find it addictive."

She pursed her glossed lips. "You think?"

Her gaze held his for a long minute. Some connection flowed between them.

Definitely addictive. He couldn't wait to see how it all played out and how those lips of hers tasted. Tristan grinned.

Jayne looked away, almost shyly. "Well, you've definitely got me intrigued."

"Intrigued is good. Not as good as naked."

She stared at a potted palm. "What about nervous?"

Not so good. He raised her chin with his fingertip. "You have nothing to be nervous about. I'm not trying to get you upstairs into a room." Not exactly. Not yet. "Tonight's about having fun. Nothing to worry about, okay?"

She nodded. "You must think I'm—"

"You're you, Jayne," he said softly. "I like being with you."

Gratitude filled her eyes.

Tristan felt an unfamiliar tug on his heart. He straightened. "Remember on the beach hike, when we talked about you playing tourist?" At her nod, he motioned to the marina office. "Tonight we're going to see a different view of San Diego."

"I haven't been on a boat in ages."

She sounded pleased. Good. "What about a gondola?"

"Seriously?"

"I told you fun was my specialty."

"Remind me never to doubt you again."

"I'll them we're here."

In the office, he gave the bottle of champagne in his pack to the desk person. She handed him a receipt for his payment and told him where they could wait.

"We have about fifteen minutes to wait," he told Jayne. "There's an area outside where we can sit."

A clear night sky greeted them. The temperature had dropped. Jayne put on her jacket.

They walked to a patio area by the marina. Italian music played from the sound system. Strands of lights provided a festive glow. A man and woman sat at one of the bistro tables holding hands. They stared into each other's eyes. Tristan didn't blame them. The setting oozed romance.

Romance could be casual and fun. Granted, a gondola ride under the stars was a little over the top, but Jayne deserved it.

He pulled out a chair for her.

She sat. "If I look past all the boats with American flags moored at the dock, we could almost be in Italy."

The couple at the other table kissed. Tristan looked at Jayne.

"A homebody who's been to Italy?" he joked. "Is that possible?"

"Well, it was eighteen years ago," she said. "I was ten."

"Vacation? Or did you live there?"

"Vacation. My dad was stationed in Crete. Or maybe it was Spain. I sometimes mix up all the different places we lived, but I remember our vacation in Italy."

"I would have done anything to been able to travel like you did when I was a kid," he said. "Aspen and St. Martens got old fast."

"No matter where else we lived, my mother always referred to San Diego as home."

"I don't really think of home as a place," Tristan admitted. "It's more a state of mind."

"Too bad we couldn't have traded places when we were kids." She glanced at the other couple, who were still making out. With pink cheeks, she focused on the table's centerpiece, an empty Chianti bottle with a candle stuck in the top. "You must have gone to a lot of trouble to arrange tonight."

She sounded too much like cautious, serious Jayne. Tristan didn't like that. "One telephone call. That's all."

"But the champagne and the boat ride and parking—"

"Before you tell me you want to split the bill, this is my treat." He leaned forward. "You cooked me dinner last week."

"You bought the ice cream."

"If I'd won, you would have bought the ice cream," he countered.

"That's true." She still sounded unconvinced.

"But...?" he prompted.

"But I'm really uncomfortable with you using a credit card to pay for all this," Jayne said in a rush. She looked up miserably. "Any of this, really. I don't want to be a wet blanket, but that takes some of the fun right out of it for me."

"You see financial irresponsibility every day at your job. I get that. I know your mom had it rough, too." Tristan fought the urge to reach across the table and take her hand. "You have to understand, Jayne, I'm not like that. Whether I use credit cards or cash, I am financially responsible. I pay my debts, okay?

She nodded gamely. "Okay."

"I'll have you know I used my debit card to pay for tonight."

She leaned forward. "Really?"

"I swear."

A dazzling smile lit up her entire face. "I'm impressed."

Tristan wondered what she'd look like if he actually paid cash. He would try that next time, because it would make her happy.

"You think you're impressed now—wait until you see the boat."

The gondolier, wearing a traditional striped shirt, dark pants, red sash at his waist and a straw hat adorned with a red ribbon, arrived. He carried an ice bucket with the bottle of champagne chilling and a tray of plump chocolate covered strawberries.

"Ready to depart on your cruise?" the gondolier asked.

"Yes." Jayne rose. "Fun's the name of the game tonight."

Tristan grinned at her enthusiasm. "You're a fast learner."

She winked. "You're a good teacher."

They followed the gondolier to a black gondola tied to a dock on the marina.

Jayne gasped. "It looks like one from Venice."

"They are imported," the gondolier said.

She smiled at Tristan. "You're right. I am impressed."

He bowed. "The evening is only beginning."

The gondolier assisted Jayne from the dock and into the gondola. The man continued holding onto her hand once she was aboard. Maybe he was just being safe, but Tristan didn't like it.

Jayne sat. The gondolier let go. Finally.

Tristan boarded and sat next to Jayne on the padded black bench. The dessert tray, champagne and glasses were set out. Italian music played.

"Help yourself to refreshments." The gondolier handed them each a blanket. "It can get chilly out on the bay."

"Thanks," Tristan said. Cozying up with Jayne sounded like a better way to keep warm.

The overhead lights from the dock shone down. The boat rocked against the deck.

Tristan dealt with the bottle of champagne while Jayne sampled a strawberry.

She sighed in satisfaction. "This is wonderful."

"Enjoy every minute," he said.

"I plan to."

The gondolier pushed off and headed to the canals of Coronado Cays.

"Simply amazing," Jayne said with a hint of wonderment. "And fun. Can't forget the fun."

"I thought you'd enjoy this."

"I love it."

Tristan smiled smugly.

"Let me guess." She studied him with an assessing gaze. "You were the kind of kid who always said 'Told ya so.'"

"Yes," he admitted.

"Then it's a good thing you were an only child."

The calmness and quiet made it seem as if they were the only ones out one the water. Even the gondolier faded into the background.

"Why is that?" he asked.

"Well, if you were the oldest child and always said 'I told you so' your younger siblings would have hated you. If you were the youngest and said it, you would have gotten beaten up by your older brothers and sisters."

"I'm happy I'm an only, then. But you're an only, too," he said. "How do you know what siblings would do?"

"I know because I used to hang out with big families every chance I got."

I would like a big family. Someday.

A family like the Stricklands, Tristan realized. Where kids, grandkids, parents, grandparents, aunts, uncles and cousins all lived within a thirty-mile radius of each other.

Guilt coated his mouth. No, he shouldn't feel guilty. Big family or not, Rich wouldn't have been good for Jayne. "I bet it was nice when you got home to your own room, where it was quiet."

"Yes, but I wouldn't have minded sharing a bedroom, and noise has never really bothered me."

Tristan wouldn't mind sharing her bedroom, either. Until he had to leave town and she found someone who could give her what she really wanted.

Way too serious. Time to lighten the mood. He poured champagne into the glasses and handed one to Jayne.

As bubbles streamed to the top, she raised her glass. "To a wonderful journey."

Tristan raised his glass. "And seeing things from a different view."

He sure was.

The first time he'd seen Jayne she'd blown him away with her natural beauty and smile. Then, when he'd learned who she was, he'd tried to view her strictly as Rich's fiancée. When she'd opened the door to her apartment he'd been shocked by her short haircut and pale face. But now he saw a beautiful woman who'd changed on the inside as much as on the outside.

Tristan tapped his glass against hers. The chime of glass on glass held on the air.

She took a sip. So did he.

The sway of the boat brought the two of them closer on the bench. Her hip pressed against him. Soft and warm. A perfect combination. Tristan liked how that felt—how she felt.

He took a bite from one of the chocolate-covered strawberries. "Delicious."

With an even wider smile on her face, Jayne took another one and bit into it. "Yes, they are."

Her lips parted, then closed around the remaining piece of her strawberry.

Tristan's groin tightened. She was really turning him on, but it was too soon for him to make his move. He didn't want to ruin the evening.

Desperate for a distraction, for distance, he removed his camera from his bag and put on a lens.

He would be an impartial observer. He was better at that than being a participant.

Turning, he took a picture of the gondolier, who stood behind them.

"And so it begins," Jayne said.

He focused on her. "Smile."

She looked over the top of her glass and stuck her tongue out.

"Please."

"Just having a little fun." Jayne smiled. "Cheese."

He hit the shutter button.

One photo opportunity after another appeared, and though taking pictures helped, nothing around him could compete with the beautiful subject seated next to him.

"You know," she said finally, "this really isn't fair."

Confused, he looked at her. "What's not fair?"

"I'm here in this brand-new fun zone," she clarified. "But you're still in your comfort zone."

"My comfort zone?"

"Behind the camera."

He stiffened. "It's my job."

She raised a brow. "Are you working tonight?"

Okay, she had a point. Tristan put the camera away. "Sorry."

She smiled. "You're forgiven."

The gondola floated by multi-million-dollar bayfront homes. Lights illuminated the balconies and patios. A few residents waved from their terraces.

"Look at those houses." Awe filled Jayne's voice. "I wonder what it would be like to live in an expensive home like that."

He knew, because his parents owned a house like that. It had never brought them happiness. "Lonely," he said before he thought.

Her eyes glowed with moonlight or compassion. He wasn't sure which. "Are you speaking from experience?" she asked.

He shrugged, his hands itching to take up his camera again. But under that soft, observant gaze he didn't dare.

"My folks have a big house," he admitted. "Too big, with just the three of us rattling inside."

"If I had a house…" She stared at the house they were passing—a two-story McMansion.

"Tell me."

She got a wistful look in her eyes. "I'd invite friends over all the time. I'd cook big meals. And at Christmas I'd have everyone I know over and the biggest Christmas tree that would fit in the living room."

That sounded pretty good to him. But when was the last time he'd been home for Christmas? He downed the rest of his champagne. "You're not going to tell me you didn't have a Christmas tree."

She flushed. "I always have a tree. But there have been a few times I've ended up on my own for the holidays."

"This year?"

She nodded. "I've always wished I lived in a house where I had enough room to invite people over for dinner or get-togethers."

"You live in a house now."

A thoughtful expression formed on her face. "I do, don't I? Molly's house is bigger than my studio apartment was, so maybe I will do that this year."

"Forget maybe," he encouraged. "Make it this year."

A part of him wanted to buy that little cottage for her as a present, even though he doubted she would accept it.

"Nothing should stop you from making that dream—any dream—a reality," he added.

"Well, first I need to learn how to cook a turkey."

Women didn't usually talk about things like this with him. The images she painted with her words appealed to him on a gut level. Something he would have never expected, given how holidays had been a sore point with Emma. He'd had no clue how to respond to his ex-wife then or to Jayne now.

"If guys can barbecue or deep-fry a turkey, I'm sure you'll have no problem," he said finally. Weak, but what else could he say?

Jayne made a face. "Deep-fried turkey sounds…I don't know…wrong."

"Ever tried a deep-fried Twinkie?"

"Uh, no."

"We'll have to add that to our list."

"List?" she asked.

"Of fun things to do."

She smiled. "Don't forget the tour of Coronado."

He tapped his head. "Already there."

The gondola made its way through the inlets and canals of the cay.

The two sat in comfortable silence, taking in the views. One by one the remaining strawberries disappeared from the tray, as did the champagne in the bottle.

Words weren't necessary. Neither were pictures.

The gondola made its way back to the resort.

Across the water of Coronado Bay, the lights of downtown San Diego glimmered.

He placed his arm around Jayne. She settled closer against him.

As a new song played, the gondolier sang in Italian. A love song, if Tristan's translation skills were correct.

"I've never been serenaded before." Jayne leaned closer against him. "Everything is just...perfect."

He'd planned on perfection. What he couldn't have planned for was the way she made him feel. The smell of her shampoo filled his nostrils. The softness pressing against him heated his blood. He wondered if she'd taste like champagne or chocolate strawberries or a combo of the two.

"I wish this didn't have to end," she said.

He knew exactly how she felt. There was no other place he wanted to be. No person he'd rather be with. "It doesn't have to end."

A part of him wasn't thinking only about tonight.

She looked up at him with a question in her eyes. Her lips parted as if to speak.

Tristan didn't give her the chance. He captured her mouth with his.

Sweet. Soft. Sexy.

She tasted like chocolate and wine and something else. Something warm and feminine. Jayne.

This was what he'd been waiting for since that first day he'd seen her in the Rose Garden. He increased the pressure of his mouth against hers.

She returned his kiss with the same hunger he felt, the same need. Her eagerness let him know she was into this as much as he was, and he wanted more.

He knew the gondolier was behind them, but Tristan didn't care.

He pulled her even closer to him. She went willingly, her breasts crushed against his chest. She buried her fingers in his hair.

Heat exploded, pulsing through his veins.

His tongue explored, tasted, and tangled with hers.

Her kiss consumed him, overloading his senses with sensation.

His heart jolted.

A sense of urgency drove him. Desire intensified. Need built within him.

He didn't just want her. He needed her. In a way he'd never needed anyone or anything before.

Warning bells sounded in his brain. Red lights flashed before his closed eyes.

The gondolier. They weren't alone.

Tristan dragged his lips from hers.

He stared at her flushed cheeks and her swollen lips. Her ragged breathing matched his own. He'd bet the fire in her eyes did, too.

A good thing they *hadn't* been alone.

Tristan was supposed to keep things light. He raked his hand through his hair. Fun and casual, remember?

But he was ready to take Jayne to bed and never let her go.

Not so casual. Not by a long shot.

Tristan reached for his camera and took more pictures. A lot more pictures.

She gave him a *what-are-you-doing*? look, but didn't say anything.

What could she say with the gondolier right there?

Tristan couldn't believe he'd gotten so caught up in kissing Jayne with an audience. He couldn't believe he'd lost control of his own feelings like that.

The gondola returned to the marina.

After tipping the gondolier, Tristan stood on the dock. No way would he allow the other guy to help Jayne off the boat. He extended his arm. Her hand clasped with his.

Her touch sent a burst of heat shooting up his arm.

Chemistry he understood, but that kiss had gone deeper than physical attraction. He didn't do deeper. He didn't even do deep.

He knew he could have fun with Jayne, but he didn't know if being casual with her was possible. He wanted it to be, but after that rock-his-world kiss he had doubts. Serious doubts.

When he'd married he hadn't had a clue what Emma had wanted from him.

But he knew exactly what Jayne wanted. What she needed. And she deserved more than he was willing to offer. Especially after what Rich had done to her.

Jayne moved carefully, with purposeful footing, until she stood on the dock. She needed to feel safe, secure. He knew that. Yet.

She looked up at Tristan. Her face was mere inches from his.

The urge to kiss her again was strong. If things had been different, if *they* had been different, he would have made his move now. But his need to protect her, to preserve his own life, made him shove his hands in his pockets and rock back on his heels. "What did you think?"

"I enjoyed the gondola ride. I liked...everything."

The kiss. The closeness.

"So did I," he said honestly.

She pulled her hand from his. "But—"

He stiffened. He hadn't been expecting her not to like any of this.

"I think I may have enjoyed myself too much. I don't want to overdose on fun my first time out."

Strange, but he actually agreed with her. "Wise girl."

Too smart for him. Too kind and genuine and open.

She bit her lip. "Maybe we should postpone our next outing."

Tristan felt an odd mix of relief and disappointment. The whole atmosphere had changed with that kiss. He didn't like it, but he didn't know how to make things go back to the way they'd been. Truth was, he needed some distance himself. "The timing couldn't be any better for postponing."

"Why is that?" she asked.

He thought about the calls he hadn't returned. All because he hadn't felt like leaving town so soon. Okay, leaving Jayne. "I've got a new assignment."

Her gaze jerked up to meet his. Lines creased her forehead. Her eyes clouded. Tristan hated how the serious Jayne could take over so quickly and completely.

"Where?" she asked.

"Central America."

CHAPTER EIGHT

Two weeks later, Jayne sat on a log at the dog park, with a silent cellphone at her ear, waiting for Molly to get back on the line. Jayne whistled to Duke and Sadie, a blue-eyed Australian Shepherd from the dog agility class, who were exploring the opposite side of the grassy fenced field. The two dogs sprinted back to her.

Jayne wished she felt as carefree and playful as the dogs, but ever since Tristan had left she'd been feeling a little…off. Oh, she hadn't retreated into the house like her mother had used to do when her father went away, and the way Jayne had done after the breakup with Rich. This time she had gone out—and even made new friends. But she couldn't stop thinking about Tristan and his kiss, a kiss that had stolen her breath and made her rethink…well, everything.

That ride on the gondola with him had opened her up to so many different possibilities—ones she'd never imagined. She felt as if her world had been turned upside down, but she had no idea how to turn it right side up again.

Truth was, Jayne wasn't sure she wanted to.

"I'm back," Molly announced.

Jayne adjusted the cellphone at her ear.

"Sorry for keeping you waiting like that." Molly's voice came across so clear, as if she were only across town instead of in another state. "Linc had a question from the contractor about the new house that needed answering right away."

"You'll be back in San Diego before you know it."

"I can't wait," her former roommate said. "Though you won't recognize me. I'm huge. I'm sure people think I'm having twins."

Molly sounded as if she was smiling. That made Jayne happy. "I saw your picture on Facebook. You look beautiful."

"Thanks." Molly laughed. "But I swear I've grown out another foot since Linc took that photo. You need to come here and see my gigantic stomach for yourself. I miss you, Jayne. Serena and Alex would love to see you, too."

The invitation hung in the air. Jayne swallowed.

"I miss you, too." She watched the dogs chase a bird. "I'll come soon."

"Before the baby arrives?"

The hope in Molly's voice pulled at Jayne's heart. "Yes. I'm sorry I haven't come sooner. I got stuck in at rut and didn't feel like doing much. But not any longer."

"What's changed?" Molly asked.

"Tristan." Jayne hoped he was well. Safe. Happy. "Though he's gone now."

"Gone? Where?"

She pressed her lips together to keep from sighing. "Central America."

"You miss him?"

Her friend knew her too well. "I do, which is really silly."

"Why silly?"

"One date and one kiss don't mean anything."

"Not usually. But this was one very romantic date and one totally toe-curling kiss," Molly reassured her. "Besides, you've spent more time than that together."

"We're just having fun," Jayne protested weakly. Tristan's kiss had made her lips throb, her heart go pitter-pat and her mind think way too serious thoughts. She'd felt herself falling hard and fast. She'd wanted—no—needed to pull back. She had to remind herself what spending time with Tristan was all about. And what it *wasn't* about—a potential long-term relationship.

"Tristan says…" She stopped.

"What?"

"He thinks I need to get out more. Let go more. Have more fun."

"Mmm. Sounds exciting."

It was.

"Maybe too exciting," Jayne admitted. "I've never been a risk taker."

"True, but is Tristan changing your mind?"

"No, I told you—we're just… I stopped looking for love after Rich."

"Be careful," Molly cautioned. "In my experience, that's when love finds you."

"I thought about that," Jayne said. "The way you and Linc got together. Alex and Wyatt. Serena and Jonas, too."

"And now you and Tristan?" The concern in Molly's voice was unmistakable. "Are things more serious than you're letting on?"

"Definitely not serious." Jayne hastened to reassure her. "Okay, I admit I imagined the two of us living in that cute fixer-upper cottage he took me to, even though he'd prefer living in a beachfront condo. But daydreaming is a long way from reality. I can fantasize with the best of them, but there's no way I can delude myself into thinking a relationship with him could ever work."

"Just remember," Molly said gently, "even if you think it couldn't be him you don't always get a lot of choice when Cupid shoots his arrow."

"Cupid better aim elsewhere, because I know it's not Tristan."

"You sound so certain."

"I am." Jayne kept an eye on the dogs. "Look at Tristan's job. He travels all over the world to take photographs. When he's not working he still likes to globetrot. I hate traveling."

"You hated living in so many different places," Molly countered. "You haven't really traveled in years."

"He'd still be gone all the time. It would be just like my parents. I could never be happy in a marriage like that."

"No, you couldn't," Molly agreed.

"Besides, even mentioning marriage is a moot point. Tristan doesn't want to get married again."

"You've put some thought into this." Molly sounded amused.

"A little. And I keep coming to the same conclusion. A relationship is out of the question."

"Does Rich have anything to do with this?"

"No," Jayne said certainly. "I'm so over Rich."

"I meant because Tristan is Rich's friend."

"Oh. Maybe at first."

"Because, as much as I hate to see you rush into anything, being Rich's friend doesn't mean Tristan's anything like him."

"I know," Jayne admitted. "But I'm still me."

"Are you sure about that?" Molly asked. "I haven't seen you in a while. For all I know this could be a rebound or a transition relationship after Rich. You and Tristan do sound very different, but he seems to make you happy—happier than you've sounded in months. That's not a bad thing, Jayne."

"Being with him does make me happy." She'd had so much fun and excitement. Except everything he made her feel was the polar opposite of what she'd been craving all these years. She'd believed stability and commitment would make her happy. Yet she couldn't deny the happiness she felt with Tristan. "I guess I just never expected to feel this way with him."

"You never do," Molly admitted. "But promise me you won't do anything rash where Tristan's concerned. Doing that can have life-altering consequences."

Jayne thought about Molly's decision to spend the night with a total stranger when they were in Las Vegas. "Things worked out great for you."

"That's because Linc and I love each other. Things could have turned out very differently," she cautioned. "You've been through so much already. I don't want you to do something that will end up hurting you."

"I promise, Moll." Jayne appreciated her friend's concern. The two dogs stared at her with expectant gleams in their eyes. "I just need to figure out a few things. That's all"

"Uh-oh. That doesn't sound like the Jayne Cavendish I know." Worry filled Molly's voice. "You've always known exactly what you want."

Jayne tossed each dog a treat. "I know."

That was the problem. The one she'd been dealing with ever since the night of the gondola ride.

Thanks to Tristan MacGregor, she no longer knew what she wanted. The future she'd dreamed about wasn't as clear.

And that scared her more than anything.

Where was Jayne?

As Tristan sat on Mrs. Whitcomb's porch, frustration gnawed at him. Two weeks away from Jayne hadn't given him the distance he'd wanted, but it had clarified his feelings for her.

He and Jayne wanted different things from life, but not every relationship had to end up at the altar. He didn't have to be her Mr. Right. He could be her Mr. Right *Now*.

"Thanks for letting me wait here for Jayne," Tristan said.

"I enjoy the company." Mrs. Whitcomb raised her carafe of coffee. "Would you like more to drink?"

The coffee was strong enough to strip barnacles from the bottom of a boat. One cup would probably keep him awake all night. "Thanks, but I still have some left."

He appreciated the neighborly hospitality and the conversation, but impatience was making it harder for him to sit still. He glanced at his watch. "Jayne's out kind of late for a work night."

"You never know what kind of traffic you'll hit these days. She and Duke will be home soon." Mrs. Whitcomb motioned to the mountainous plate of chocolate chip and oatmeal raisin cookies. "Have more cookies."

"I will." Tristan took three. "I spent the last two weeks eating random meals. A few were non-edible, too."

"Lou would have liked you. He had an adventurous soul, too."

The affection in Mrs. Whitcomb's voice for her late husband made Tristan believe they were one of the rare couples that had found something special. The vast majority wasn't so lucky.

He'd spent his adulthood exploring the unknown. He'd never backed down from a challenge no matter what the risk—sometimes to life and limb. He'd thought he knew what relationships were about, but nothing had prepared him for this. For Jayne. She was both unknown and a risk, but he was ready for both.

He hoped she would accept what he was offering.

A dark four-door sedan with tinted windows pulled to the curb. The non-descript car reminded him of a vehicle from a detective show on television.

The police? Jayne?

His concern quadrupled. Tristan stood.

Mrs. Whitcomb used the porch rail to help her stand. "See—I told you they would be home soon."

They?

A few seconds later Jayne got out of the car, placed a black and white dog with butterfly ears and an ostrich plume tail on the ground and shut the passenger door.

His heart beat faster.

He'd taken the J-peg files of her with him on his assignment, but photos couldn't capture the essence of Jayne. Or the way her jeans cupped her bottom perfectly.

Another car door slammed.

A man, probably about his age, walked around the front of the car to the sidewalk where Jayne waited. Every one of Tristan's muscles tensed. A blue-eyed dog followed at the strange guy's heels. With his casually styled blond hair, wrinkled navy polo shirt and khaki shorts, he looked an awfully lot like Rich. Except for that carefully nondescript car.

Jayne's type?

Tristan set his jaw. "Who's that?"

"Kenny... I can't remember his last name. He attends Duke's dog agility class." Mrs. Whitcomb said. "He had an errand to run, so Jayne offered to take the dogs to the park. I think Duke has a crush on Kenny's dog Sadie."

Jayne laughed at something the guy said.

Tristan thought Sadie's owner had a crush on Jayne. He clenched his hands.

Mrs. Whitcomb sighed. "The two of them look so good together."

The guy touched the small of Jayne's back. The possessive touch had Tristan ready to hurdle the porch rail and tackle Kenny head-on.

"That guy does *not* look good with Jayne."

"I was talking about the dogs."

Tristan charged down the steps. He positioned himself in front of Mrs. Whitcomb's porch. No way could Jayne miss seeing him or Kenny get around him.

Duke scampered ahead of them. The sissy dog barked at Tristan. He had to be careful not to step on the damn thing.

Jayne looked toward the house.

Damn, she was gorgeous. Not just her face and her body, but her heart.

He knew the minute she saw him. Her smile widened and spread all the way to her eyes.

His breath caught in his throat.

"Tristan." Jayne quickened her steps, and he met her halfway down the front walk. "You're back."

"I am." He sized up the blond guy and nodded in acknowledgment. "Tristan MacGregor."

"Kenny Robertson," the other man introduced himself. He looked from Tristan, to Mrs. Whitcomb on the porch, to Jayne, obviously waiting for an explanation.

Let him wonder, Tristan thought.

"Tristan's a friend of mine," Jayne said.

The word "friend" grated like fingernails against chalkboard. Tristan had thought that kiss on the gondola had made it clear he wanted to be more than friends. Guess not.

She continued. "He's a photojournalist and has been out of the country on an assignment."

Kenny's stance relaxed slightly. He offered his hand. "Nice to meet a friend of Jayne's."

Tristan bared his teeth in a smile, feeling like a dog with a bone. He tightened his grip. Kenny did the same.

Jayne's brow creased as she apparently picked up on the unspoken tension. "Tristan is the one who told me to stop being such a homebody and get out of the house more."

"Right before he left the country?" Kenny asked.

"I was only gone two weeks," Tristan said.

"Well, it's been a great two weeks." The guy made puppy eyes at Jayne. "Jayne is an amazing social director."

Tristan raised his eyebrows. "Social director?"

She nodded, her cheeks pink with enthusiasm. Or maybe embarrassment. "For the dog agility class. I've been organizing get-togethers and events for people outside of class."

"You'd be good at that," Tristan said.

"Jayne's great at it," Kenny said.

The color on her cheeks deepened. "It's given me something to do."

"I have something to do. It's past Duke's bedtime," Mrs. Whitcomb announced. "We're going to call it a night."

"I'd better get going, too." Kenny rubbed Sadie's head. "Work tomorrow."

"Me, too," Jayne said.

Tristan stood his ground. He wasn't going anywhere. "Nice to meet you, Kenny."

The guy nodded. "See you at the next agility class, Jayne. Let me know if you want to carpool again."

Carpool? Tristan fought the urge to grimace. Saving gas money would appeal to Jayne. The guy probably knew it and was trying to earn bonus points.

"I will," she said.

After a chorus of goodnights, Tristan was finally alone with Jayne. About time. "Come with me to my car. I have to get something out of the trunk."

She fell into step next to him.

"So you got out of the house?" he said.

"I've decided I'm not quite the homebody I thought I was." Her smile dazzled Tristan. "Tonight Molly invited to me to visit Las Vegas again, and this time I said yes."

"Impressive."

Pride gleamed in her eyes. "It's a step in the right direction."

"I'd say you've taken a few steps forward." He pulled out the bag that contained the present he'd purchased for her on his trip. "Traveling to Vegas. Becoming a social director."

"Yes, you're right." Her confidence appealed to him. "I've enjoyed meeting some new people. Dog people, but they're very nice."

"Like Kenny?"

She nodded. "Making new friends has been good."

That word again. This time applied to Kenny. Tristan didn't mind so much. He opened the trunk.

"So good, in fact," she continued, "I've decided not to get a roommate."

Tristan closed his trunk. He was fine with her decision. It would make it easier for her to move out of the bungalow if she bought a place of her own. "You sound sure about that."

"I am pretty sure," she said. "So when did you get back?"

"Today. I wanted to see you right away." He stared into her warm, clear eyes. "I missed you, Jayne."

"I missed you, too."

"Good."

"I'm not so sure."

Tristan realized she wasn't smiling. He noticed Mrs. Whitcomb peeking out her window. "Why don't we talk about this inside?"

Jayne nodded, and he followed her into the house.

He set the bag on the coffee table. "Tell me what you're not sure about."

She looked up, down, around. Everywhere but at him.

Not a good sign.

He had a pretty good idea what the problem was. "It's me?"

Her startled gaze met his. "It's not you. It's me."

That caught him off guard. "You?"

Jayne nodded, her eyes clouded with unease. She wrung her hands. "After what happened with Rich I don't trust my judgment when it comes to relationships. Men."

Damn. Tristan wanted to go back and make things right. "It's not your fault Rich wasn't ready for marriage."

Lines creased her forehead. "But I thought… He said… I was so sure…"

"This is a completely different situation." Tristan wanted to take away her uncertainty. "Rich didn't know what he wanted. I've been honest with you from the beginning about what I want and don't want."

"You have."

"You know what you need to know about me," Tristan said firmly.

Her anxious face looked up at him. "Do I?"

A tense silence filled the living room.

He thought about his role in her and Rich's breakup. Telling her the truth would only make her mistrust herself more. Yet Tristan had learned from his first marriage the importance of honesty in a relationship if you wanted to share a future.

"Let's talk about what happened with Rich."

"Let's not," Jayne said without any hesitation. "The past is in the past, remember? I don't need to talk about it. I don't want to talk about it."

This wasn't the first time she'd talked about putting the past behind her. "Fine."

What else could he say? Do?

Nothing good would come of the discussion anyway. Honesty was important, but it wouldn't change anything between them. He and Jayne weren't looking to share a future. They didn't want the same future.

Happily-right-now.

That was all Tristan could offer Jayne.

He hoped it would be enough for her.

Tristan picked up the bag from the table and handed it to her. "I brought you something from Honduras."

"The bowl and candlesticks are lovely." Warmth flowed through Jayne as she sat at the kitchen table with Tristan. The black and white handcrafted Lenca Pottery was her new centerpiece. "Thank you."

Tristan placed his spoon in his ice cream bowl. "I thought they might come in handy when you have people over for those big dinners you mentioned."

The gift pleased Jayne, but confused her, too. "You seem to know me pretty well."

He shrugged. "I saw them in a window and thought of you."

His present symbolized hearth and home, gatherings of family and friends. All the things he claimed not to want or care about. "They're perfect."

Tristan's mouth curved into an easy smile. His lips looked soft and welcoming, the kind meant for long, slow, hot kisses. The kind of kisses he gave.

She felt a flutter in her chest. "You'll have to come to one of my dinners."

"Just tell me when."

Jayne reached out and touched one of the matching candlesticks with her fingertips.

"In case you were wondering—" his eyes twinkled with amusement "—I paid cash. You must be rubbing off on me."

His lighthearted tone teased, but his words sparked a connection. Jayne could sense something drawing them together as if they were magnets. Perhaps opposites did attract.

"That makes them even more special," she said. "I wish I had something to give you."

The amusement sharpened. "You gave me ice cream."

"I definitely got the better end of the deal."

Tristan laughed. "You could give me a proper welcome home."

Before she could respond, he'd scooted his chair closer. He wrapped his arms around her in a comfortable embrace.

An intoxicating aroma of soap and male surrounded her.

A sigh threatened to escape.

Her hands splayed over his back. Underneath the fabric of his button-down shirt she felt muscular ridges against her palms and fingers.

Welcome home had never felt so good.

Jayne felt right at home. Safe. Secure. A way she hadn't felt in months. A way she'd never expected to feel with Tristan.

Maybe she did know all she needed to know about him.

She knew Tristan didn't believe in forever, but he made her happy. Molly was right about that. He'd also brought fun back into Jayne's life. Excitement, too. Nothing wrong with that.

He could give her more of that.

She knew better than to expect anything else from him. She wouldn't allow herself to get carried away like she had before.

She couldn't.

Because Tristan wanted fun, not forever.

And that, Jayne realized, was okay with her for now.

His warm breath fanned her neck. "It's good to see you."

Her pulse quickened. "Yes. I mean I'm pleased to see you, not me."

"I know what you mean." Tristan pulled her closer. "It feels even better to hold you."

Her chest pressed against his. So solid and strong. The pounding of his heart matched her own. "Uh-huh."

She glanced up to find him gazing down at her. His eyes so intent. His lips so close.

Her mouth went dry.

He was going to kiss her. Heaven help her, she wanted him to kiss her.

Tristan lowered his mouth to hers until their lips touched. A spark arced through her from the point of contact.

She gasped, but he didn't back away. Nor did she.

She closed her eyes and let sensation take over. The same way she had on the gondola. Only this time they were alone. There was no one serenading them, no one watching them. She liked this much better.

He moved his lips against hers, softly and deliberately, testing and tasting.

Hot ice cream. An oxymoron, yes, but that was what Tristan's kiss tasted like tonight, and it would be her new favorite flavor.

Eager for more, she leaned into him.

His lips moved expertly over hers. She found a sense of belonging, the home she'd always dreamed about. His jean-clad leg pressed into her. His tongue explored and danced with hers. Her insides hummed.

Tristan kissed her so thoroughly, so completely.

She wanted him to keep kissing her. She needed him to keep kissing her.

Slowly he drew the kiss to an end and sat back.

Her lips sizzled.

She wished the kiss hadn't ended.

Jayne didn't know how long they sat at the table staring at each other. He looked the way she felt.

Happy. Turned-on. Hungry for more.

She took a deep breath. "So…"

"So let's go to Vegas."

She stared at him, stunned. Images of the chapel where Serena had eloped and the hotel where Molly had spent the night swirled through Jayne's mind. "Vegas?"

He nodded. "You said you were going. Let's go together. You can see your friends. They can meet me and tell you how great I am for you."

She laughed, relieved to know what he was thinking, but a tad disappointed, too. "You think that's what they'll say?"

"Yep."

His confidence didn't surprise her. She wished some of it would rub off on her. "You're really up for this?"

"I really am," he said, without the slightest hesitation. "Call Molly and see if this weekend works."

That sounded dangerous and wild and so appealing—because Jayne hadn't done anything like that since saying yes to Rich's marriage proposal after only a month of dating. She wanted to know that things could work out better than her ill-fated engagement. "Just like that?"

"Yes, Jayne," Tristan said.

The way he said her name made her feel all tingly. Her tummy felt like a butterfly house.

Promise me you won't do anything rash where Tristan's concerned.

Jayne remembered Molly's words as well as the fun her three friends had had in Vegas.

Uh-oh. A weekend out of town in a place known as Sin City. They would spend a night or two in a hotel. Tristan might assume—would probably assume—that meant staying in the same room and sharing the same...

Her insides quivered. "I—"

"What's wrong?"

She raised her chin. "Why do you think anything's wrong?"

He touched her forehead with his fingertip. "These little lines show up when you're either thinking or getting serious about something."

His perception disturbed her. "I didn't know that."

"So tell me what's on your mind."

Blurting the word "sex" might not be the best move. She needed to figure out a subtle way to broach the subject. "I'm not sure I'm ready for that much fun."

"I'm not following you."

She thought about the queen-sized bed in her bedroom. They didn't have to fly to Vegas to... "I don't believe in casual sex."

The words rushed out like the overspill from a floodgate.

Subtle, Jayne. Real subtle.

"What I mean is there's no one else I'd rather go to Vegas with, but I'm not... I would prefer it if we had separate beds. Or rooms. I like you. A lot. And I really like kissing you. But I don't want to rush into anything. Or do something we might regret. I understand if you're disappointed and don't want to go now."

Feeling like an old-fashioned maiden, she stared at the centerpiece he'd given to her. Maybe she should forget the entire thing, get a dog, and resign herself to being single the rest of her life.

"Two rooms are fine, Jayne," he said gently. "There are lots of ways for us to have fun that have nothing to do with sex."

Her gaze met his in gratitude. "Thank you."

"So Vegas is a go?"

The anticipation in his voice buzzed through her. Jayne would love to hear what her friends thought of Tristan, too, though she thought they might warn her off him. "It's a go."

His smile crinkled the corners of his eyes, and her breath caught in her throat. "You get in touch with your friends and see if this weekend works for them. If not, find dates that do. Then I'll make all the travel arrangements. This trip is on me."

"That's really generous of you, but Alex's husband Wyatt owns a hotel. I'm sure we can get rooms—"

"Let me take care of it, Jayne."

"But airfare and a hotel," she countered. "It's going to be expensive."

"I can afford it."

She started to speak, then stopped. She nibbled her lip. *Shut up, Jayne. Shut up.*

But her training and her conscience wouldn't let her stay quiet. "Are you sure? Because a lot of people feel that using credit—"

"Jayne." He scooted his chair closer. He took her hands in his strong, reassuring clasp. "I can afford it."

"If you were super-rich you could."

He nodded.

Oh, man. She almost slid off her chair.

"My dad has a plane we can use, too."

All the pieces fell together. Paying off his credit card each month. Working for his father. Growing up in a big house. Traveling the globe to take photographs.

He was serious. He *was* rich. Really rich.

Even if he didn't wear designer clothing or drive a flashy car or live...

She sighed. "I'm an idiot."

"No, you're not."

"We're even more different than I thought." Tristan had grown up with a silver spoon. Hers had been plastic. "And here I was, giving you financial advice."

He squeezed her hand reassuringly. "You gave me very good advice that I needed to hear."

Jayne appreciated his words, and the sincerity in his eyes. She smiled. "Well, you're making sure I have the fun I need."

"We're a good team."

She nodded. Team, not couple. She just had to remember that.

CHAPTER NINE

THURSDAY night, Tristan sat in a local sports bar, waiting for Rich. A Los Angeles Lakers basketball game played on the large screen television.

The game couldn't hold his attention.

Face it, not much had held his attention this past week.

Tomorrow he was leaving for Vegas with Jayne.

He took a swig from his pint of beer.

He wanted her friends to give him the thumbs-up. Maybe then Jayne would trust her own judgment. Maybe she would trust *him*. And maybe she would want them to get…closer.

A lot closer.

He'd asked her out tonight, but she had the dog agility class with Duke. Duke and Kenny. So Tristan had accepted Rich's invitation to hang out and watch the game. They hadn't talked in weeks. It was time—past time—to come clean to his oldest friend about seeing Jayne.

"Chicken wings and fries." Rich put the food on the table and sat across from Tristan. "Seems like old times. The only things missing are a couple of beautiful babes checking us out."

Unease inched down Tristan's spine. He reached for a couple of fries. "How's the wedding planning going?"

"Okay, I guess."

A feeling of *déjà vu* washed over him. Not again. "You met someone?"

Rich nodded.

Damn. "I'm not going down this road with you again, bud."

Rich squared his shoulders. "It's different this time. She's different."

Annoyance flared. "I don't care if she's a *Sports Illustrated* swimsuit model. You can't do this again."

"I haven't done anything."

Yet. The unspoken word floated between them.

"But you want to," Tristan said.

"Hell, yeah," Rich admitted. "She's hot."

"You said the same thing about Deidre. Smokin' was your exact word."

Rich shrugged.

"Don't hurt Deidre the way you hurt Jayne."

"You played a part in hurting Jayne, too, dude."

"But I wasn't the one screwing around on my fiancée," Tristan ripped out the words. "You messed with her heart and her confidence."

"I would have never proposed if she would have just slept with me."

"Huh?"

"Jayne doesn't believe in casual sex. I thought if we were engaged she would finally give in and say yes."

Every single one of Tristan's muscles tensed. "You asked Jayne to marry you to get her in the sack?"

Rich shrugged and flashed his *hey-buddy* grin. "It seemed like a good idea at the time."

Tristan shook his head. "For you, maybe."

"Well, it didn't work out like I planned," Rich admitted. "She wanted to wait until our wedding night to do the deed."

That explained the short engagement. "It was still a jerk move."

Rich downed the remainder of his beer while Tristan's gut churned.

Poor Jayne. While she'd been planning her wedding and dreaming of her happily-ever-after, Rich had been thinking only of having sex with her.

Tristan shifted uncomfortably, reminded of his own plans for the weekend. He was hoping for the chance to sweep Jayne off her feet and into bed himself. But at least he wasn't dangling the together-forever carrot in front of her the way Rich had.

Images of Jayne sprang into Tristan's mind. The excitement on her face at the cottage. The wistful yearning in her voice on the gondola ride. The passion in her eyes right before he'd kissed her.

What the hell was he thinking?

"I don't want to see you make another mistake, Rich. Marriage is a serious business." The words sounded hollow to Tristan. He reached for more fries. "My marriage failed because I wasn't ready then. You're not ready now."

Rich pressed his lips together.

"I'm not going to be there to watch your back this time," Tristan said. "Break it off with Deidre the way you should have with Jayne."

"I'll think about it."

The Lakers scored a three-point shot. The crowd in the bar cheered.

"Looks like they could go all the way this year," Rich said. "Wanna try to score tickets to a game this weekend?"

"I'll be in Vegas."

"Without me?"

Tristan shrugged.

"There's gotta be a woman involved," Rich said. "Who is she?"

This was the moment of truth. No woman had ever come before their friendship, let alone threatened it. Tristan inhaled slowly, as if waiting an extra five seconds to answer would make a difference.

"Jayne," he said finally. "We're leaving tomorrow."

Rich's mouth gaped. "*My* Jayne?"

"She hasn't been yours for a while."

"Is this payback for when I dated Julia Sommers after she broke up with you?"

Julia had been the captain of the cheer team, a pretty, ditzy blonde who'd ended up dating the entire basketball team. Tristan had forgotten about her until now. "That was back in high school, bud."

Rich studied him. "But you don't like Jayne."

"I have always liked her, but I knew better than to put the moves on my best friend's fiancée."

"Is it serious?"

Tristan hesitated before answering.

"Who am I kidding?" Rich said before Tristan could answer. "You don't do serious."

The words bristled, but a cold knot formed in the pit of his stomach at the truth behind them.

Tristan didn't do serious.

He knew it. Rich knew it. And so did Jayne.

Inside the suite at McKendrick's, Tristan flipped a ten to the bellman clad in a hunter green uniform with gold trim.

"Thank you, sir. Please let me know if you need anything else." The attendant pocketed the bill with a smile. "Enjoy your stay at McKendrick's."

The bellman left, closing the door behind him.

Tristan looked at the two bags sitting next to each other on the living room floor. Soon the bags would be carried into separate bedrooms. Not ideal, but better than the thought of them in completely different hotel rooms. Or back in San Diego.

"Wow, this place is so huge." Jayne pirouetted like a ballerina across the carpet.

Seeing her so carefree and happy brought a grin to his face. She was definitely embracing the concept of having fun.

As she spun, the hem of her little black dress clung to her thighs and hips, making her curves and already long legs seem almost criminal. Her strappy sandals only added to the alluring picture. His hands itched for his camera, and for her.

He was determined not to take advantage of her the way Rich had. Tristan wasn't hiding behind a careless marriage proposal. Jayne knew exactly where he stood when it came to relationships. He'd been open and honest. If she was game for more fun, then so was he.

She stopped twirling and faced him, her cheeks flushed and her eyes sparkling.

Jayne was—in a word—stunning. Forget about traveling not appealing to her. Tristan had never seen her so radiant, so animated before. He wanted to show her the amazing sights he'd seen all over the world. He wanted to kiss her on all seven continents, across every time zone.

She trailed her fingertips along the back of an elegantly upholstered chair. "I've never stayed in such a luxurious room before."

Tristan glanced around. It was nice as far as hotels went.

"I guess you must be used to nice hotels like this," she added.

He shrugged. "I've stayed in some pretty crappy places on assignment, especially when I was first starting out."

Jayne drew her brows together. "But I thought you had money."

"I didn't gain access to my trust fund until I turned thirty," he explained. "Now that I have, I've continued to support myself. But I remember being married and trying to establish myself as a photojournalist. It was a struggle to make ends meet."

"I didn't think you knew what it meant to struggle."

He laughed. "I do. Well, did."

She started to speak, but stopped herself.

"What?"

"It's just…the more time I spend with you, the more I realize how much I don't know about you."

"By the end of this weekend you should know most everything."

Jayne's smile could have lit up the Las Vegas strip. It sure was lighting up him.

"I hope so," she said.

The anticipation in her voice sent a burst of heat rocketing through his veins. He'd never been so physically attracted to a woman before, yet he wanted all of Jayne—not only her body. "I want to know everything about you, too."

She struck a pose. "What you see is what you get."

He flashed her his most charming grin. "I like what I see. I'm sure I'll enjoy whatever I get."

She swirled into his arms and kissed him firmly, quickly, on the lips. "This is all you're going to get right now."

Before he could embrace her fully and kiss her again she twirled away. A hint of her strawberry and wildflower scent lingered.

The coy look in her eyes told him she knew he wanted more. Okay, he was a guy. Of course he wanted more. But Tristan didn't know whether to be proud of Jayne for taking control of the situation or annoyed at her for getting away from him. Thinking about his conversation with Rich last night, Tristan settled on proud.

"It's enough." He winked. "For now."

Laughter spilled from her lips. "Separate bedrooms, remember?"

"I'm the one who booked the rooms, remember?"

"I haven't forgotten."

His gaze locked on hers. "Neither have I."

The air sizzled with attraction. The desire in her eyes held him captive. He didn't know how long they stood there, staring at each other, but he didn't care. Being with Jayne was all that mattered.

Too soon, she broke the contact.

She walked to the bar where a large fruit basket and a bottle of wine sat. "Look at this."

Tristan hadn't ordered anything. "See if there's a card."

Jayne opened the small envelope, pulled out a card and read.

Jayne and Tristan
Enjoy your weekend at McKendrick's! Let us know if you need anything!
Love
Alex and Wyatt

"Wyatt McKendrick is my friend Alex's husband," Jayne explained. "He offered Alex a job while we were staying here. Her life has never been the same, but she has no regrets."

"Lucky lady," Tristan said. "Not many can say that."

"True, but all three of my friends have no regrets over what happened during that wild weekend."

"Are you ready to have your own wild weekend?" he asked.

She raised her chin. "Well, I'm here. That's a pretty big step for me."

"I know." He strode to her side, raised her hand to his lips and kissed the top of it. Her skin was soft and smooth. "I'm going to make sure you have no regrets."

"So far, so good."

His heart beat faster. He wanted to make sure she never forgot this weekend. Whatever it took, he would do it. Or... not do it.

"We should probably get ready for tonight." She pulled her hand away. "Which bedroom would you like?"

Whichever one you choose. He pushed the thought from his mind. "I don't care."

He didn't. Knowing she was in bed in the same suite was going to make sleep impossible.

"The room on the left can be yours," Jayne said. "The room on the right will be mine."

She was so damn cute. Tristan smiled. "You sound like you're dividing spoils after a war."

Jayne straightened. "Just making sure we each know where we'll be sleeping."

"The living area can be neutral territory. If you don't like sleeping alone, there's a sofabed out here we can share."

With wide eyes she stared at the sofa, then back at him.

Tristan didn't know if she was tempted or upset or nervous. Only one of them appealed to him. The others made him feel like a jerk after he'd told her no regrets.

"Kidding," he joked. "I have no idea if the sofa turns into a bed or not."

She cast him a mischievous glance through her lashes. "Maybe you should find out."

Definitely tempted. His heart skipped a beat. Okay, three.

Humor glinted in her eyes. "I'm kidding too. I know you're a man of your word."

A man of his word.

Just like...

I'm a man of my word. I'm the only one she's got. Maybe once the wedding's over things will get better.

Rich.

A lump the size of a neon lightbulb lodged in Tristan's throat.

Rich prided himself on being a man of his word, even if that meant being a jerk and hurting Jayne.

Tristan didn't want to be lumped into that category. Rich's marriage proposal hadn't been his friend's smartest move, and Tristan knew better than to try and steal home this weekend. He wasn't about to start rounding the bases without a clear signal from Jayne.

He could never be what she wanted, needed, deserved. He couldn't give her the fairytale and forever, but he could make sure she had the time of her life this weekend.

And Tristan would.

A DJ spun a mix of indie rock and eighties songs. A handsome bartender concocted cocktails with improbable names. A manicurist provided demonstrations.

Jayne was as far away from home as she could imagine, but there was nowhere she'd rather be right now than in the fifties-beauty-salon-themed bar in downtown Las Vegas.

Alex sat on an old-style hairdryer seat and raised a martini glass filled with a Blue Rinse. She looked beautiful in a magenta dress and matching heels. Not quite so serious or professional as the practical suits she wore to work at McKendrick's. "To the best friends in the world."

Jayne lifted her drink, a Drop Dead Gorgeous—a delicious combination of vodka, pineapple juice and an energy drink. Molly and Serena joined in the toast, too.

The flash from Tristan's camera lit up their table. He hadn't wanted to join them for drinks, but had paid for theirs. He'd asked if he could take a few pictures before leaving them alone for some much needed girl-time.

He took candid shots of them as they chatted and sipped their drinks. Though she was delighted to finally be with her friends, it was all Jayne could do not to stare at him. His short-sleeved green shirt was tucked into his khaki pants. His leather shoes had been recently polished. He wore a belt.

Comfortable, yet stylish. Smart-casual. And once again he had the look down.

"How did we miss coming here the first time we were all in town?" Molly drank a mocktail—a non-alcoholic version of a Pink Blush martini. The name matched the glow of her cheeks. She rested her left hand on her tunic-covered belly. "It's kitschy, but hip."

"Totally hipster." Serena drank a Platinum Blonde. Wearing a purple cocktail dress, she looked like the same artsy type who'd lived in San Diego, except she seemed a little more… serious and aware of her surroundings. She waved to people she recognized and said hello to those she didn't. "I just love 'Martinis & Manicures' night."

Jayne struggled to take it all in. The change in her friends. The change in her since Tristan had re-entered her life. She sipped her drink.

Tristan stopped circling the table. "I have enough pictures for now."

As he stood next to her, her pulse quickened. She couldn't forget the change in the way she thought of him—Rich's best man to friend to date to boyfriend.

Possible boyfriend, she amended.

Jayne knew better than to get ahead of herself. She had been a little too carefree and flirty at the suite, but the way he'd kept looking at her had made her feel sexy and desirable. She liked how that felt.

"Thank you for being such beautiful subjects," he said.

The four of them thanked him for their cocktails.

"The driver knows what time our dinner reservations are, in case you ladies forget to check the clock." Tristan kissed Jayne on the lips. The brief kiss claimed her attention and nearly made her spill her drink on her lap. "Have fun."

Another kiss would be fun. She took a sip of her drink instead.

He swung his camera pack over his shoulder and walked out. As soon as he was gone she looked to her friends, hoping they would reassure her that seeing Tristan was a good idea. "So, what do you think?"

"Definitely hot," Alex said.

Molly nodded. "Gorgeous."

"Total eye candy. He looks more like a model than a photographer." Serena laughed. "I can't believe you actually thought you could be just friends with a man like that."

Jayne remembered what he'd said about the sofabed in neutral territory. Tempted? Yes. Which was why she would lock her door tonight. Not to keep Tristan out, but to remind herself she needed to stay in her own room. "Our friendship is evolving into something more, but the emphasis is on good clean fun."

At least that was what Jayne kept telling herself. Back at the suite, she hadn't been so sure anymore.

Molly tucked her dark hair behind her ears. "Spending a weekend in Las Vegas with a guy is a little more serious than what you're making it out to be."

"We're spending a weekend with all of you," Jayne clarified.

"And we're so glad you're here," Alex said.

"I feel better having met Tristan." Serena picked up her drink. "It's obvious the guy adores you."

Molly grinned. "I'd say the feeling's mutual."

"I agree." Alex stared over her martini glass. "I've never seen you look this happy before."

Jayne had never felt happier. She should probably be more concerned than she was. Tristan must be rubbing off on her. Or maybe knowing the relationship wouldn't last forever took some of the pressure off. Whatever it was, her affection for him grew every day. So did her respect.

"Tristan's great. Wonderful. Insert any other positive adjective here," Jayne admitted. "But I'm not about to jump into anything like I did with Rich."

"Rich said all the right things," Alex said. "He fooled all of us, Jayne. But it seems like Tristan is *doing* all the right things."

Serena nodded. "Words are easy to say, but actions take a lot more effort and work."

Jayne thought about how fluttery she felt when she was with him, or talking to him on the phone, or…" Tristan has been good for me—getting me out of the house and doing things."

"Clean things?" Alex asked.

Serena winked. "Or dirty ones?"

"Either can be fun," Molly added.

The implication of their words sent excitement rippling through Jayne. Not that she would. Or he… Strike that. Tristan probably would. She sighed. "You guys never used to talk like this. Is it marriage?"

Alex drew her brows together. "I'm not sure if it's marriage per se…"

"It's probably the sex," Serena said with a grin.

Molly nodded. "You and Tristan—?"

"Are sleeping in separate bedrooms," Jayne finished for her. She felt a pang at her heart, remembering the tension in the suite. He'd wanted to kiss her. She'd wanted him to kiss her, too. But she had to be smart about this. About him.

"They're staying in one of McKendrick's two bedroom suites," Alex added. "The guy has excellent taste."

"Of course he does," Molly agreed. "He's dating our Jayne."

"Casually dating." Jayne took a sip of her drink. "Having fun is one thing, but getting serious with a man who wants such a different future than I do would be a huge mistake. I learned my lesson with Rich."

Rich had seemed like the perfect match. Everything she'd ever wanted he could have given her. Tristan, however, was all wrong for her. And yet…

Jayne could imagine herself with him.

She liked the person she was around him, even though the way she'd acted when they'd arrived at the suite had been all heart and no head. Maybe she had loosened up a little too much and put the wrong amount of emphasis on having fun.

"Coming to Las Vegas with Tristan might have been premature. A little caution might be prudent," Jayne decided.

"Nothing wrong with being cautious," Alex said.

"If I had been cautious I wouldn't have married Jonas," Serena countered.

Molly patted her belly. "And I wouldn't be having this baby and be married to Linc."

"I could say the same thing about me and Wyatt," Alex said. "But we're not Jayne."

"And Tristan isn't like your husbands." Jayne didn't have to think hard to remind herself of all the reasons he was wrong for her. "I'd be crazy to fall head over heels with a guy who doesn't believe in commitment."

If only he did believe…

She stared in her drink.

"The fact Tristan travels even more than your father did can't help," Serena, also a military brat, said shrewdly.

Jayne nodded, acknowledging the truth. "Tristan does travel a lot, but when he was in Honduras I knew he would be coming back. I never felt that kind of certainty when my father went away. But I know it would get old fast."

Once that happened, the resentment would start to build. She'd seen it with her parents. Her mother had wanted her father home. He hadn't been able to wait to leave again. The disagreements had become arguments. The arguments had become battles. She wouldn't want Tristan to be unhappy.

"Tristan might have to go away for his work, but I don't think he's going anywhere else," Molly said. "He didn't take his eyes off you. This bar is full of women and he saw only one. You."

"Tristan hasn't given me a reason not to trust him," Jayne admitted. "But Rich didn't, either."

"Be cautious, then," Serena said. "But remember love knows no logic."

Molly laughed. "Just look at the three of us."

"That's true. You should make sure Tristan knows where you're coming from," Alex added. "The guy really does seem to like you, and men aren't known to slow down when they want something. Or someone."

"Thank you, but he knows exactly where I stand." Too bad Jayne felt as if she were standing on shaky ground. "I'm trying to be smarter this time."

At least that was her plan. She wasn't too confident of its execution so far.

Serena smiled at her. "Well, I think you're doing great."

"I agree," Alex said.

"Me, too," Molly chimed in.

The three women sitting at the table with Jayne meant the world to her. They had shared the highs and the lows. She would trust them with her life. But Tristan saw something in her they didn't. He pushed her, challenged her to be more.

She'd taken a gamble coming to Vegas with him. Still, that didn't mean she should bet the farm on their relationship. She knew he wanted more from her. A part of her wanted that, too. Except...

Tristan couldn't give her the future she dreamed about—stability, a home, marriage and a family.

Yet he was one of the sweetest, hottest men she knew. He was also a man of his word. He'd always been honest with her.

The truth was, she'd come to care for him. She cared for him a lot.

But even if she trusted him, could she trust these new feelings of hers?

CHAPTER TEN

AT SPARKLE, *the rooftop* restaurant at McKendrick's, Jayne sat at a round table with Tristan, her friends and their husbands. The view from the thirtieth floor mesmerized her. A crescent moon shone high in the desert sky. The clear night provided views for miles, from the dazzling neon of the strip to the small twinkling lights of homes farther away.

"What are you looking at?" Tristan asked, sitting next to her.

"All those little homes, far off in the distance."

"A home doesn't have to be so far off," he said.

Her heart beat a little faster.

When she was with Tristan, Jayne felt as if she was already home. No picket fence, leaded-glass built-ins or hardwood floors required.

What had he said?

I don't really think of home as a place. It's more a state of mind.

She was beginning to understand what he meant.

"Make your dream come true, Jayne," he encouraged, his voice low.

His warm breath practically caressed her earlobe. She could hardly breathe.

Her dreams—ones she'd held close to her heart since she was a little girl—were suddenly changing. Maybe emotion was leading her astray again. Jayne only knew that however her dreams evolved she wanted someone like Tristan to share them with.

Those feelings clogged her throat.

Jayne stared at the flickering white votives surrounding a green hydrangea centerpiece. Servers, dressed in black pants and crisp white shirts, circled the linen-covered table, clearing the dishes from the delicious meal.

Linc, Molly's husband, removed his suit jacket and rolled up his sleeves.

"Your friends are great," Tristan whispered. "I'm enjoying myself."

"I'm glad." She was surprised how well he fit in, like the final piece of a jigsaw puzzle. "They like you."

"Told ya so."

A smile tugged on her lips. "Yes, you did."

The tenderness in his gaze brought a sigh to her lips. He hadn't physically touched her, but Jayne could feel his imprint on her heart.

Jayne felt so comfortable with him tonight, as if they were in a relationship with feelings and a future.

But she knew it had to be the situation. Surrounded by three happy, contented couples, it would be easy for her to read more into Tristan's presence, into his words.

She wouldn't allow herself to do that.

Daydreaming was bad enough.

She focused on the people at the table.

Conversation flowed as easily as the wine, though Molly wasn't drinking. Neither was Linc.

Jayne sipped her red wine as Molly entertained them with stories of her efforts to get Linc to help her fill out a baby journal for the baby before they had gotten married.

Molly shook her head. "He actually said the book shouldn't be called *Memories For Your Baby*, but *What Every Hacker Wants To Know About You*."

Everyone laughed, but Tristan looked at Jayne with a question in his eyes. "Linc is the CEO of his own software security company," she explained quietly.

"Got it."

"In my defense." Linc's smile reached all the way to his eyes. "They *do* ask for some very personal information."

"Because it's for a baby book." Molly touched her stomach. "Your baby."

"Our baby," Linc countered.

"Yes, he is." She had changed physically with her pregnancy, but Jayne loved how Molly also appeared to have loosened up, and she laughed more freely than she'd used to.

Tristan raised his wine glass. "Here's to a healthy baby."

Molly beamed. "Thank you."

"It's great you could join us, Tristan," Serena said.

"Thanks for having me," he replied. "It's nice to put faces with names."

"We're glad you could get away," Molly said. "I understand you travel a lot?"

Uh-oh. Jayne wondered if an interrogation was about to begin.

"I'm a photojournalist."

"Wire service or newspaper?" asked Wyatt, with his arm around Alex.

"Freelance," Tristan said.

Linc set his water glass on the table. "Competitive field."

"It is," Tristan agreed. "But that just means I have to be that much better than anyone else."

Jayne exchanged looks with her three friends. Serena winked at the guys being guys, but Jayne found it interesting to watch Tristan holding his own during the testosterone driven exchange.

"Tristan took pictures of us at the bar earlier," Serena said. "I can't wait to see them."

Jonas' brow furrowed at his wife's words. "I thought that was girls'-only time."

Tristan flashed a charming smile, the kind that made Jayne go weak in the knees. "I was simply the photographer."

Wyatt McKendrick refilled Jayne's wine glass. He cut an imposing figure at the table, with his designer suit, black hair, chiseled features and electric green eyes. The staff buzzed around like perfect worker bees. No doubt having the boss there meant extra special service. "Alex tells me this is your first time at Sparkle, Jayne?"

"Yes, we ended up eating at the Bistro Lizette when we stayed here in June."

"We wanted to eat here, though," Serena said.

"But none of us could afford it then," Alex added.

Jayne still couldn't. She looked at Tristan. He had money, just like her friends did now.

Underneath the table, he clasped her hand and gave a reassuring squeeze. She squeezed back.

Wyatt raised a dark brow and stared at his wife. "Are you trying to tell me our prices are too high?"

"Nope," Alex said, without a moment's hesitation. A grin lit up her face. "Just that our bank accounts were too small."

The way Alex no longer felt the need to count to ten before she said anything pleased Jayne. Her friend could be herself and not hold back and worry about the consequences anymore.

Jayne expected Tristan to let go of her hand, but he laced his fingers with hers, as if settling in for the long haul. As if he wouldn't drop her as soon as an interesting assignment beckoned from some faraway land.

If only...

No, that wasn't fair.

Tristan had a job to do, one that had nothing to do with her.

He rubbed her hand with his thumb. Maybe she needed to stop thinking so much and just enjoy the moment.

"I'm glad I finally got the chance to eat here. It's...amazing," Jayne said, distracted by Tristan, who kept playing with her fingers. "Definitely worth the wait."

His thigh pressed against hers.

"Sparkle is just another jewel in the McKendrick's crown." Jonas Benjamin had removed his suit jacket, and finally loosened his tie. "I hope to see Wyatt and Alex's portfolio of properties expand in the not-so-distant future."

"In case you haven't figured it out, Tristan," Serena said, "my husband is the Mayor of Las Vegas, and sometimes forgets he's not at City Hall."

Jonas put his arm around her. "But you love me anyway."

"Yes, I do." She kissed him. "Even if you won't get an 'I Heart Las Vegas' tattoo. You might appeal to another constituency if you did that."

Jonas laughed at her joke. "I'll consider a tattoo when you start wearing pastel jackets with matching skirts and a strand of pearls."

Serena smiled mischievously. "Let's not forget a hat, gloves, and coordinating handbag."

"Those would be excellent touches, my dear," Jonas teased.

Her eyes sparkled. "Except we both know I'll never be a typical politician's wife."

He pulled her close. "And I wouldn't have it any other way."

Serena might not have thought she'd ever fall for a buttoned-down lawyer turned politician, but the two were a perfect match. Jayne had noticed the changes in her friend at the bar earlier.

"Opposites attract," Tristan said.

Linc smoothed Molly's hair. "I'd say they do."

She stared up at her husband with adoring eyes. "Most definitely."

"I'd agree," Alex said.

"Me, too." Wyatt hugged Alex. "There's no way I could let a ten-pound chocolate bar go uneaten for months."

"Now you're just humoring me," Alex teased. "He would never eat it."

"No, but I'd share it with you," Wyatt said.

Jonas laughed. "No question about us being opposites here, but it works."

Everything Jayne had wanted for her three best friends—love, happiness and health—had come to them. Everything she'd gone through—betrayal, heartbreak, pain—had been worth it to see this right now. Jayne wouldn't change anything.

She stared at Tristan.

Everything had worked out for the best.

Serena looked from Tristan to Jayne. "I guess opposites really do attract."

Jayne's cheeks warmed. She would love to be married like her friends, but she knew that wasn't what Tristan wanted.

She waited for him to say something, to voice the distance between them or emphasize the casual fun factor.

"Jayne and I are opposites." He brought their clasped hands up onto the table. "But we're helping each other see different points of view. It's all been good. I'm sure it will continue to be."

Her heart lodged in her throat. A warm feeling of contentment flowed through her. His words gave her hope.

Each of her friends had found the perfect mate, a partner for life. She wanted what Alex, Molly and Serena had found here in Las Vegas. Not the white picket fence and the nine-to-five husband, but someone to cherish who would cherish her. That had always been Jayne's dream.

One true love. A happily-ever-after.

That much was still a part of her dreams.

She looked down at her fingers entwined with his.

It wasn't Tristan's dream.

But maybe, just maybe, it could be.

* * *

Tristan stood with Jayne in the atrium lobby of McKendrick's. Light jazz played from speakers hidden in columns. An elderly couple in matching red, white and blue jackets shuffled across the marble floor. A bride and groom sipped champagne from crystal flutes and accepted congratulations from strangers.

Jayne's friends had called it a night, but Tristan knew heading to the suite this early might not be his smartest move. Not when he couldn't keep his hands off her.

Time to make plans for the rest of the evening. Fast.

"The night's still young," he said.

"I'm game."

Her mischievous smile hinted at a challenge and heated his blood.

A small group of people entered the lobby. Women wearing floor-length gowns, teetering on stilettos and sporting bling, clung to the arms of men in tuxedos. An almost toxic mixture of expensive perfumes hung in the air after they passed.

"Let's go to the Bellagio," he suggested.

"I'm not much of a gambler," Jayne admitted. "I can't understand why anyone would want to throw money away like that."

"We aren't going to gamble," he said, almost desperately. Going up to their suite would be the biggest gamble they could take right now. "The Bellagio is America's playground. There's plenty to do that has nothing to do with gambling."

Three gray-haired women dressed in various shades of purple and red and wearing outrageous hats sashayed and kicked in unison across the lobby, as if they were Rockettes.

"Lead the way," Jayne said with a grin. "I know I'm in good hands tonight."

He wanted her in *his* hands. Tristan swallowed.

"Come on," he said.

A taxi dropped them off at the Bellagio as one of the choreographed water fountain shows in the lake was coming to an end. Tristan led her into the lobby. He noticed men staring at her and brought her closer to him.

Jayne stared up at two thousand colorful blown glass flowers hanging from the ceiling. "Gorgeous."

He glanced her way. "Very."

The heels of her sandals kept her from moving too quickly across the marble and mosaic flooring. Tristan slowed his pace so his steps matched hers. "This way."

"You know your way around." She sounded curious. "Come here often?"

"Actually, yes," he admitted.

Piano music played from a nearby lounge.

"I think that's the piano bar where Molly met Linc." Jayne peered inside. "Serena met Jonas in another lounge here somewhere."

"Sounds like your friends hit the jackpot."

"They sure did." A contented smile settled on Jayne's lips. "Lady Luck was smiling down on them."

"She could be doing the same thing with you."

Jayne's gaze met his. She blushed. "I hope so."

So did Tristan.

"This is the Conservatory and Botanical Gardens," he said as they walked through the entrance into a huge glass dome.

Colorful blossoms, green plants and flowering trees surrounded a large fountain. A sweet floral fragrance hung on the air as they followed the path around.

She looked around. "It's incredible."

He nodded. "I've gained a new appreciation for flowers."

"Any reason?" she asked.

"Meeting you in the Rose Garden at Balboa Park."

Jayne smiled. "That kind of sweet-talk could have consequences."

"I'll take my chances."

Even though he knew the odds of getting burned were high.

"Risk-taker," she teased.

"How about you? Ready to take a chance?" he asked.

"Not completely, but I wouldn't mind dipping my toe in to test the water."

A start. He would take it.

"I want to show you another place." He exited out a door on the left. "Close your eyes."

Jayne did. "I trust you."

Her confident tone made him uneasy. He tugged at his suddenly too tight shirt collar.

"We'll be there in a minute." He led her up to the patisserie and stationed her in front of the chocolate shop's masterpiece. "Okay, open your eyes."

Jayne stared at the twenty-seven-foot, floor-to-ceiling fountain. Behind a wall of glass melted white, milk and dark chocolate cascaded down, pooling and streaming until it reached the bottom.

"Wow," she said.

"Up for some chocolate?"

"I think I must have died and gone to heaven."

"I thought you would like this."

"I do," she admitted. "I love it. Everything. Thank you."

She rose on her tiptoes and brushed her lips across his.

His heart lurched. His pulse raced.

That was when he knew.

He was falling for her. Hell, he'd already fallen.

Tristan gazed into her sparkling eyes and saw stars. White picket fence stars. Two point four children stars. Happily-ever-after stars.

What was he doing? What had he done?

His stomach clenched.

He had fallen in love with her. That was bad.

She was falling for him. That was unforgivable.

He'd already given his best shot at being what someone else needed him to be. He hadn't been able to do it.

He wasn't going to lie to Jayne the way Rich had. She trusted him to be honest with her. Tristan wasn't going to fool himself, either.

No matter how he felt about her, no matter how she might feel about him, he was not what she needed.

The sooner she realized it, the better.

Standing in the elevator on the way up to their suite, Jayne tingled all over. She'd never felt so courted, so cherished, so treasured, so…loved. She clutched the bag of chocolates Tristan had bought for Mrs. Whitcomb.

"Everything has been so perfect tonight. Dessert at the patisserie was the icing on the cake. Thank you."

"You deserve it, Jayne." He looked closely at her with an unreadable expression on his face. "You deserve…"

Her heart pounded in her ears. Maybe he would…

"You have chocolate by your mouth," he said, catching her off-guard.

Self-conscious, Jayne looked at her reflection in the shiny gold-walled elevator. "Where?"

"A tiny smear," he said. "By the edge of your lip."

Jayne licked the side of her mouth with her tongue. "Did I get it?"

"Not yet." Using his thumb, he wiped the corner of her mouth. His thumb pad was rough, his touch slow and intimate, almost a caress.

Jayne's breath caught in her throat.

Sensation surged from her lips through the rest of her. Heat pulsed through her veins.

His gaze met hers. "All gone."

She wanted to grasp the fleeting moment before it disappeared.

The heat in his eyes held her captive. She melted, feeling all liquid and warm, like the chocolate from the fountain.

A single thought, a lone desire, rang through her mind. *Kiss me.*

That was what she wanted. A kiss. Kisses.

He continued staring at her. Her eyes. Her mouth.

Her own need shocked Jayne. She'd never felt this way before.

Kiss me. Kiss me. Kiss me.

Tristan took a quick breath. But he didn't kiss her.

Of course not.

He was keeping his word. He might not be the kind of man to get on bended knee, declare his undying love and propose, but he had her best interests at heart. That made her love him even more.

Love him?

Jayne's breath caught in her throat.

She loved him.

Her heart swelled with emotion.

Somehow, somewhere, she'd fallen in love with Tristan MacGregor.

The realization didn't scare her as much as she'd thought it would.

She wanted this.

She wanted him.

And that left her only one choice.

To kiss him herself.

Rising on tiptoe, Jayne balanced herself with her hands flat against his smooth cotton shirt, against his strong, warm chest, above his rapidly thudding heart.

He stiffened in surprise.

Dizzy with her own daring, she pressed her mouth to his.

The touch of Jayne's lips shocked his system like a jolt of caffeine. The taste of her—chocolate, sweet and rich—went to his head faster than the wine he'd drunk with dinner.

Bad move, his brain yelled to him. Bad idea. He should end this now.

He couldn't be what she needed. He couldn't... Oh, hell.

The way her lips moved over his, devouring him as if he were the slice of chocolate cake she'd eaten earlier, ignited a flame inside him. His brain shut off. His body flared to life.

Her kiss made it hard to think, impossible to do the right thing.

Tristan wanted her.

Even if he knew he shouldn't.

A sexy moan escaped her lips. The sound pushed him closer to the edge. He struggled to hang on. "Jayne..."

She leaned into him, pushing him back against the wall of the elevator. Her hips rocked against his.

Her mouth pressed harder against his, taking the kiss deeper. Her lips moved over his with impatience, hunger. Her tongue tasted, explored, plundered.

Jayne's aggressiveness surprised him. She'd seemed more kitten than man-eating tiger. But he had no complaints. He loved her daring.

He loved *her*.

She wove her fingers through his hair.

A hot ache built low in his gut. He needed her closer.

He wrapped his arms around her until her soft breasts pressed against him. She went willingly. That only stoked the fire. He wanted to be inside her. He slipped his thigh between her legs.

He ran his hand along her smooth thigh. The hem of her dress inched upward.

His control slipped another notch. Maybe ten.

Back away, Tristan told himself. Pretty soon he wasn't going to want to stop. He didn't want to stop now.

Ding.

Jayne jerked away from him, her eyes wide and her lips swollen. She smoothed her dress back into place, her fingers trembling. He felt a pang deep in his belly.

The elevator doors opened. A middle-aged couple stepped toward the car.

"Going up?" the man in a Denver Broncos jersey asked.

"Yes," Tristan said.

"Oops." The woman, wearing a navy blue tracksuit, smiled. "I must have pressed the wrong button. Sorry about that."

So was Tristan. But a part of him was thankful. He knew where that kiss had been leading. Where he'd wanted it to go.

The elevator doors closed. He saw Jayne's reflection. Her pink flushed cheeks. The rapid rise and fall of her chest.

She looked so sexy, so vulnerable. He wanted to take her in his arms again and kiss her. The way he felt about her right now, kisses would never be enough.

But he couldn't afford to do anything else. Truth was, he couldn't even afford more kisses.

Tristan touched her shoulder, wanting to reassure her.

The shy invitation in the depths of her eyes nearly bowled him over.

"Want to take this into neutral territory?" she asked.

Tristan could have what he wanted. He could have her.

But there was no thrill of victory. No shot of pride. No fist-pumping.

If Tristan took what he wanted from Jayne he would be no better than Rich.

Strike that. Tristan would be worse, because he actually loved her. He loved her quick smile, her generous nature and her rock-his-world kisses. He loved her.

No matter what Jayne thought she wanted, he knew better. She was awash in a glow of emotion and sensation. Her heart was leading her someplace she'd said she didn't want to go. He had to protect her. He had to protect himself from acting on the way he felt.

No regrets.

For either one of them.

CHAPTER ELEVEN

Keep moving, Jayne thought as she and Tristan entered the suite. If she slowed down to think about what she was doing— what they were about to do—she might stop altogether.

And she didn't want to stop.

She never wanted this night to end. Euphoria bubbled over. She felt giddy, as if her smile was permanently fixed upon her face. Her pulse leaped with excitement.

Jayne floated to the sofa. She could barely feel her feet touch the carpet. The air seemed charged with electricity, with attraction. The anticipation was almost unbearable.

Her heart stuttered with love and nerves and desire.

She reached the sofa.

Neutral territory.

Her insides tingled. She felt breathless.

Tristan stood on the other side of the living room, his eyes, dark and intent, never leaving her for a moment.

He was so handsome, so strong, so caring.

A dizzying shiver of wanting coursed through her. She fought an overwhelming need to be next to him. Soon, very soon.

Holding his gaze, Jayne sat.

He took a step forward, then stopped. "You want something to drink?"

Her heart fluttered wildly.

Had he forgotten his comment about the sofa? How could he forget?

No, she realized. A warm glow settled the wild beating of her heart. He was trying to do the right thing. He was a man of his word. Her feelings for him intensified. How could she not love him for looking out for her?

She gave him a shaky smile. "Not a drink."

Come here. Her eyes implored him. *Don't make me say it.*

"Well, then," he said. "Maybe we should call it a night."

Oh, no. That wasn't how she wanted tonight to end.

Jayne couldn't say what she wanted, but she could show him.

With unfamiliar bravado, she tapped the cushion next to her.

He didn't move, didn't take the hint.

Her heart raced uncomfortably.

She loved him. She wanted this. She wanted him.

What was she doing wrong?

Maybe she should try what had worked in the elevator.

Jayne rose, crossed the room and stood in front of him. He was so tall and his shoulders so wide.

A sense of urgency drove her. Her body ached for his touch.

She placed her palms on his chest.

Heat emanated from him. His heart pounded. She felt his breath hitch.

Good, he was turned on, too. Her pulse-rate skyrocketed.

She ran her hands up his chest until they reached his shoulders, put her arms around his neck and pressed her breasts against his hard chest. She waited for him to pull her into an embrace.

The muscles beneath her palms tensed. "What are you doing, Jayne?"

He still hadn't wrapped his arms around her.

"I'm trying to seduce you," she admitted flirtatiously. "But I don't seem to be getting very far."

"You're doing great, but..." His warm breath fanned her face. "Why are you doing it? I can't give you what you need."

All she needed was him. Him, and the feeling of being loved, valued, cherished that he gave her.

Her confidence spiraled upward. "All I need right now is a little cooperation."

He laughed, and for a moment she thought everything would be all right.

And then he took her arms from around his neck and pressed a tender kiss in each palm. "Jayne...you deserve more than cooperation."

He knew her dreams. She'd told him what she had wanted with Rich. What she hadn't told Tristan was that *what* she felt for him, with him, was so much greater than what she'd ever felt for Rich.

"I'm not expecting any promises," she said sincerely.

"I can't be a suburban husband."

"I'm not asking you to marry me. I'm not asking for anything." She glanced over Tristan's shoulder at her open bedroom door. "Well, except..."

Her cheeks burned at her brazenness, at the implication.

"I can't," he said firmly.

She looked at him confused. "Can't?"

The silence stretched between them.

He stared at her as if he were photographing her with his eyes, but then broke the contact. He kissed each of her fingers—ten perfect, heart-wrenching kisses—and let go of her hands.

He glanced at the door to his bedroom and sucked in a long breath. The unfamiliar vulnerability in his eyes squeezed her heart. "This isn't what you want."

Well, no. She wanted everything. The magic and forever. She wanted him in her life for always. But if she couldn't have always she would gladly take tonight.

Jayne raised her chin. "Yes, it is."

"You don't really know me."

"Yes, I do," she countered. But his words stirred old doubts about her judgment. As much to reassure herself as him, she said, "I know enough. You're kind. You're giving. You've helped me get a life. You've shown me what's possible and how I can make my dreams come true. My friends like you, too."

"Sweetheart, I'm overwhelmed. Flattered. But—"

"You're looking out for me," she said. "That's all I need to know. I trust you."

"You shouldn't. You don't know what I'm capable of."

A chill shivered down her spine. Could she have misread him that badly? The way she'd misjudged Rich when he'd claimed he wanted to marry her? "I thought you wanted this, too?"

"Not now."

His rejection stung, but she refused to let go of her hopes for the evening, her trust in him.

"I don't understand." She was lost in a confusing haze of feelings and desire. His words, his abrupt change of mood, made no sense. Maybe he just needed reassurance. "You were honest about what you want. I'm fine with that. I don't need forever. I'm ready to accept your terms. Here. Now."

A vein throbbed at his jaw. "Jayne…"

Why wasn't he taking her into his arms and kissing her? She couldn't believe she was throwing herself at him and he didn't want her. Doubts swirled, gnawing at her confidence. "What's wrong with you? What wrong with *me*?"

"It's not you. You're perfect," he said gently. "It's me, Jayne."

"It's you I want."

"You deserve more than me."

A beat passed. And another.

She couldn't take it any longer. She didn't want to beg. "Tristan…"

His features tightened. His gaze clouded. "I'm the one who sent the text message telling you to go to Rich's apartment for a surprise."

Her mouth gaped. She felt an instant squeezing hurt. Jayne took a step back. "What?"

She waited for Tristan to say something—anything.

Instead, he strode to the bar and poured her the drink she hadn't needed before. "Rich wouldn't tell you about him and Deidre and he made me promise I wouldn't, either. So I had to find another way to make sure you found out before the wedding."

"No." Jayne's knees quivered. She staggered back until she bumped into a chair. She sat before her legs buckled. "You're just saying that. I don't know why, but…"

Tristan gave her a glass of red wine.

Her hands trembled so badly she had to set the glass on the end table.

"It's true," Tristan said.

True.

The word seared her heart. "How…?"

"I was waiting for Rich in the dressing room of the tuxedo shop when I saw your name flash on the display screen of his cell. I knew he was seeing Deidre later, so I took your call to be a sign and sent you the text message."

Emotion tightened her throat. "I never understood why Rich felt the need to orchestrate me finding out that way. It was so cruel, so heartless. Wondering why he'd planned the breakup that way kept me awake for weeks. Now I realize it wasn't him at all."

"If I had it to do over again—" Tristan shoved his hands in his pockets "—I would do it differently."

The words crashed down on her. Not just the words. The evening. Her hopes.

Tears pricked her eyes, but she kept them in check.

How could this be happening?

Jayne loved Tristan. She had trusted him. She had felt safe with him. She had believed he would be good to her. But she'd been wrong. Dead wrong. "So would I."

"I know you're upset."

Grief ripped through her. She wanted to throw up. "You have no idea how I feel right now."

"You're right. I don't." Red stained his tanned face. "What I did was cruel, but not heartless. I was desperate to stop the wedding. I knew you'd be miserable if you married Rich."

"You're Rich's best friend." She struggled to hold herself together. She felt as if she would lose it any second. She squared her shoulders. "Why did you care about me?"

"Because I liked you."

"You didn't know me."

"We had this same discussion that day I returned your postcard," he reminded her.

Jayne remembered.

You don't like me.

I like you.

No, you don't.

Yes, I do.

The only reason you're here is for Grace.

Grace asked me to stop by, but that doesn't mean I don't want to be here.

Jayne's mind reeled. She tried to force her confused emotions into order so she could understand. "But you were Rich's best man."

"Let me show you." Tristan removed his wallet, pulled out a photograph and handed it to her. "See yourself through my lens. Through my eyes."

The picture was of her. She wore a pink blouse and skirt. Pink rose blooms surrounded her.

"I saw you standing there and that was it. I fell. Hard." The honesty in his voice cut through her pain and confusion. "I took your picture, lots of them. This one is my favorite."

Jayne stared at the photograph. It was as if the camera had worked magic. The lighting and soft focus made her look so pretty.

Not the camera. Tristan had made her look that way.

Something clicked in her mind. Her heart drummed. She looked from the picture to him. "You liked me?"

Tristan nodded. "From that first day. The very first moment, really. But then I found out you were marrying my best friend, and I was his best man, *his* best friend, so I had to keep my distance."

It all made sense now. Tristan's glares had been a disguise. His silence had been his shield. But that knowledge didn't ease the pain in her heart.

A hot tear slipped from the corner of her eye. She wiped it away.

He continued. "When I learned Rich was cheating on you, I couldn't stand to look you in the eye."

But Tristan was looking her in the eye now, with a combination of regret and affection that splintered her broken heart even more.

She blinked back the rest of the tears stinging her eyes and threatening to fall. "All I see is a woman who's been fooled again by a man she trusted—by her own foolish hopes and bad judgment."

"Jayne—"

"I trusted you." Her voice cracked.

"Trust yourself."

No, she couldn't. And that, Jayne realized with sudden clarity, hurt most of all.

Her judgment wasn't simply bad. It was totally off. Totally wrong. Just as it had been with her father. Just as it had been with Rich.

And once more her heart would pay the price.

A lump burned in her throat. "Why didn't you tell me this before?"

The muscle ticked in Tristan's jaw again. "Because you wanted to put the past behind you. And I just wanted you."

He had tried to tell her, she remembered now. She pressed her fingers to her aching forehead. She didn't know what to think, what to say.

The silence intensified the tension between them.

Jayne's chest hurt. She could barely breathe. Emotion and hurt raged inside her.

She let go of the photograph. It floated to the carpet.

And I just wanted you.

"Too late for that," she said in a choked voice. "I could never love someone, trust myself to someone, who could hurt me like that—who could make me question my own judgment again."

"I understand."

And he did, Jayne realized with another tear of her heart. That was why he had stopped things from going too far tonight.

"For what it's worth," Tristan said quietly, "I'm sorry. You'll never know how sorry I am."

His words ripped at her heart. At her soul.

"Me, too," she admitted, her voice as raw as her heart. "But sorry isn't going to change anything."

Tristan sat up all night. Waiting for something. The dawn. A sign. Jayne.

But she'd retreated into her bedroom and locked the door.

He hadn't seen her.

Not that seeing her would have made any difference.

Sorry isn't going to change anything.

He stood at the window of their suite, watching the brilliant desert sunrise take over the lights of the strip, feeling cold and empty. He couldn't justify what he'd done to her or to himself. He wasn't going to be like Rich and make excuses.

Tristan had made his own choices. He would accept the consequences.

But he wanted to know she was okay.

He stared as the new day broke, surrounded by lonely silence, assailed by regret.

As time passed his concern over Jayne increased, until he couldn't stand still any longer. He paced across the living room.

Tristan noticed Jayne's picture lying on the carpet. He picked it up and stared at the image. His chest constricted.

No reason to keep this any longer.

He walked to the trashcan. His hand hovered over it, ready to drop the picture inside. But his fingers wouldn't let go.

Truth was, he didn't want to let go.

He put the picture back in his wallet.

Tristan glanced at the digital clock. Eight o'clock.

He resumed his pacing.

Shouldn't she be up by now? Unless she'd had as restless a night as he had?

Last night he'd heard voices—a phone call to one of her girlfriends, perhaps?—and other sounds, until the room had fallen silent around four in the morning.

Should he check on her? Should he call her friends?

The lock on Jayne's door clicked.

He froze.

As the door opened, Jayne appeared.

She'd been crying. Her red and puffy eyes made his heart hurt even more. The dark circles under her eyes and pale skin told him she hadn't slept much, either.

A heaviness settled in the center of his chest.

He'd done this to her.

Tristan felt like an even bigger jerk.

She held her packed bag in her hand.

"You're leaving?" he said hoarsely.

Jayne nodded.

Don't go, he thought.

But what had he expected her to do? He'd hurt her in the worst possible way. He couldn't offer her any reason to stay. She deserved better.

"When?" he asked.

"After lunch." Her voice sounded strained. "I'm going to spend some time with my friends first."

Tristan hated how she wouldn't look him in the eyes. His already aching heart seemed to split open. He wanted to make things better between them. He wanted her to want him again. He wanted her to love him. Instead, all he could do was help her leave.

"I'll call a cab to take you to the airport when you're ready," he said. "My father's plane will be waiting for you."

Tristan would call the pilot so he could make the necessary preparations.

Her lower lip quivered slightly. "No."

The one word spoke volumes. Disappointment weighed down on him. "Then I'll buy you a plane ticket."

She inhaled deeply. "I'll buy my own plane ticket."

"You can't afford it."

The knuckles of the hand holding onto her bag turned white. "If I can afford a down payment on a house, I can afford a damn plane ticket."

He admired her flash of spirit. He fought the urge to go to her, to take her in his arms and make this all better. But she didn't want that.

She didn't want him.

Tristan stiffened. "I don't want you spending your money. I got you here. I'll get you home."

She met his gaze.

The raw hurt he saw in her eyes made him grab the back of the chair. He loved her. He hadn't wanted it to turn out this way. His fingers dug into the upholstery.

"I'm tired of you telling me what I want and what I need." Her voice never wavered. "I can take care of myself."

"Let me," he offered sincerely. "Let me give you this much."

"You can't give me what I need."

Tristan flinched. She'd tossed his words back at him. Rightly so, he realized.

With her bag in hand, she walked quickly across the living room to the front door.

He wanted to stop her, but he didn't. He couldn't.

She deserved her exit line, at least.

Jayne opened the door.

Wait, Tristan wanted to yell.

She didn't glance back. She didn't even say goodbye.

Instead Jayne Cavendish stepped out of the suite and out of his life.

"Are you sure you want to leave today?" Alex sat on the floor of her penthouse apartment in front of a coffee table covered with dishes: fruit kabobs, pastries, bagels, yogurt and quiche. "We can get you another room to stay in."

"Or you can stay with one of us," Molly suggested.

Serena nodded. "We have plenty of room at our place."

"Thanks, but I want to go home." Jayne forced the words through her raw throat. Her heart ached. The sight of all that food made her churning stomach lurch. Couldn't eat, couldn't sleep. Must be… No. She struggled to keep her voice steady. "I'll be back soon, though. We need to throw Molly a baby shower."

"Don't think of me right now." Molly sat on the couch. Rocky, her Jack Russell terrier, slept at her feet. "I'm not going anywhere. Just getting bigger."

Everyone laughed.

Jayne pasted a smile on her stiff lips.

"Wyatt's made arrangements for you to fly back on the McKendrick's jet," Alex said.

"Thank you so much."

"It needs to be in Los Angeles on Monday anyway, so it's no big deal." Alex held a mug of coffee. "There's a car to take you to the airport whenever you're ready."

Jayne swallowed around the lump in her throat. "I really appreciate all you're doing for me."

"You don't have to put on a front, Jayne," Serena said softly. "It's okay to cry."

"It is, Jayne." Alex handed over the box of unused tissues. "We're well stocked."

She'd told them about what had happened with Tristan after the dinner at Sparkle. Her friends had offered her support, friendship, hugs and chocolate. She loved them so much.

"Thanks, but I cried buckets last night. I'm all cried out today." Right now Jayne clung to a fragile thread of self-control. The endless wallowing and pity parties after her breakup with Rich had taken their toll not only on her emotions but also her health. "I don't want a repeat performance of the hysterics after Rich."

Even though this hurts more.

She hadn't been engaged to Tristan, but she loved him.

Had loved him. Had thought she loved him. She didn't trust her own judgment anymore.

"Rich." Serena groaned. "If it had been him last night, he would have slingshot your panties across the suite before you could blink."

"Rich was a hound," Alex said. "Even if he was your fiancé."

"A hound and a liar," Serena added.

Molly adjusted the pillow behind her back. "I guess the two men aren't that different after all."

"I liked Tristan," Alex admitted. "Well, before he hurt you."

"Jonas thought he was a nice guy," Serena said.

Molly frowned. "Why are we saying nice things about Tristan? He hurt Jayne."

Fairness compelled Jayne to speak. "Tristan was trying not to hurt me last night. Otherwise he would have taken advantage of the situation, of me."

Alex and Serena exchanged glances over the coffee table.

Serena's eyes darkened. "Sounds like you still have feelings for him."

"I do," Jayne admitted. "I thought I'd wake up this morning and feel differently, but I don't. Still, I let my desire cloud my judgment. With Rich I wanted happily-ever-after. With Tristan I wanted love."

Alex leaned forward. "If you love him—"

"We were never going to have a forever kind of relationship. That's not what he's looking for," Jayne interrupted. She wasn't supposed to have been looking for that, either. "Besides, he never told me he loved me."

"Unlike Rich," Molly said. "Didn't he tell you that early on?"

"The third date," Jayne answered. Rich had declared his love over and over again, but besides proposing he never had shown it. Tristan had never mentioned love, but his actions last night proved she meant something to him.

Her breath caught in her throat.

No, Tristan couldn't love her. If he did, he would have said something.

The apartment door opened. Wyatt walked in with an envelope in his hand. "This was left at the front desk for Jayne."

She took the envelope with a tentative hand. Her name was scrawled on the front in sharp, bold letters. She opened the flap with a mix of anticipation and dread.

"What does it say?" Serena asked.

Jayne removed the contents. "It's a plane ticket. A first-class plane ticket to San Diego."

Molly rubbed her lower back. "That's impressive."

"He wants to take care of you, Jayne," Wyatt said.

Even after she'd asked him not to, Tristan was still trying to take care of her. Jayne noticed a yellow Post-It note stuck to the ticket.

You deserve more.

The words stabbed at her broken heart. She fought to control her swirling emotions.

She reread the three words. *You deserve more.*

This time the words didn't bother her as much. She reread the note a third time. *You deserve more.*

She remembered what he had said to her.

You deserve more than cooperation. You deserve more than me. You deserve more.

Maybe Tristan was right. Maybe she did deserve more.

Maybe it was time for her to finally get what she deserved.

Jayne straightened.

She just needed to figure out what that might be.

CHAPTER TWELVE

ON HER knees in the garden, Jayne attacked the new weeds sprouting between the rows of carrot and radish plants. It was only seventy-two degrees, nothing like the hot summer temperatures Southern California was known for, but still the winter sun beat down on her. A trickle of sweat ran between her breasts and soaked her bra.

But she was keeping occupied. Work and gardening and the dog agility class and finding excuses not to go out with Kenny kept her busy.

She didn't think about Tristan at all.

Well, not much.

Only every, oh, minute or so.

She swiped her forearm across her forehead.

When the phone rang it was a relief. Maybe it was Alex or Molly or Serena. Jayne's friends called her every day. Or maybe it was…

Tristan.

She jumped from her knees and bolted to the house.

Stupid. He wouldn't call. It was over. And yet…

No matter how many times Jayne told herself it was over with Tristan, a part of her still wanted him to call or show up at her door. She had no idea what she would say or do, but she just wanted to see him again.

"Hello?" she said, sounding breathless from the sprint inside.

"Hi, Jayne," a familiar male voice said. "It's Rich."

Reality hit with a thud. She clutched the phone receiver. Nine months ago a call from Rich would have made her happy. Even after the wedding fiasco she'd prayed for him to call, to apologize, to explain. Now it was too late. Anticlimactic. A bit of an annoyance, actually. "Why are you calling me?"

Silence filled the line.

"I talked to Tristan," Rich said finally. "He told me I was a real jerk."

"Yes."

"That I hurt you."

She had been hurt. Hurt and furious. Now she was relieved she hadn't married him. "So?"

"Tristan told me I wasn't ready to get married. To you or anybody else. I want you to know I should have listened to him."

Tristan had been looking out for her—then and now. She bit her lip. "Sounds like you're listening now."

"Yeah," Rich admitted. "His friendship matters to me. Whether you believe it or not, what you think about me matters, too. I called to apologize, Jayne. I'm sorry. I really am."

Okay, this was really, really awkward. She didn't need his apology. And yet she was glad to clear the air, close the book. She was glad the man she'd thought she'd loved had finally grown up to acknowledge what he'd done.

"It's okay, Rich." She had let go of the past. It was time to live now and be ready for the future. "I'm over it. I've moved on.

"Yeah, I heard," Rich said. "Good luck with that."

She wasn't sure what he was talking about. "Uh, thanks."

"You know, Tristan is a really good guy."

"I know."

"Loyal," Rich said earnestly. "He stuck by me when I was acting like a complete idiot."

Tristan must have told Rich about them. Not that it mattered now. "Friends do that."

"So…I'll see you around?"

"Probably not."

"When Tristan gets back from his assignment in Africa," Rich clarified.

Her heart beat faster.

Africa. Was that why Tristan hadn't called or stopped by? Because he was out of the country?

Hope sprang to life.

No, she wasn't going to delude herself again. She deserved more than that. She deserved—

"Jayne…?" Rich said.

"I'm here. Sure," she said, distracted by her thoughts. "See you then."

"Bye." Rich hung up.

Jayne set the phone on the counter and returned to the garden, walking as if she were in a dream. She knelt on the pad and picked up the trowel.

She had what she wanted all wrong.

It wasn't the husband. A man like Rich could have offered her the trappings—but not love and fidelity.

It wasn't the house. Oh, she still planned to submit her offer on the fixer-upper cottage tomorrow, but four walls and a roof, no matter how quaint or perfect, didn't make a home.

She dug in the dirt, the desire to plant roots stronger than ever.

A house and husband were the beginning, not the end.

Jayne knew with pulse-pounding certainty what she wanted, what she deserved.

She wanted a man who saw her and loved her for who she was. A man who was not afraid to say he loved her and commit. A man who would work to build a life with her.

That man was out there somewhere.

She wished it could be Tristan. She wanted it to be him. But, she realized with a pang, he had never given her a chance. Never given her the choice.

Jayne remembered what Tristan had said to her that first day he'd shown up on her doorstep.

You don't have to look. Someone will find you.

She hoped he was right.

In Botswana, Tristan aimed his camera at the traditional Tswana village gathering. The men sat apart from the women in the courtyard where the festivities took place. The bright colors of the women's aprons contrasted with brown houses that looked more like thatched huts. He hit the shutter button.

This was the kind of assignment he thrived upon. He'd flown into Johannesburg and had been traveling around Botswana for the past week to take photographs for an article about the impact of tourism on economic development. Not as exciting or dangerous as being embedded with a battalion in the Middle East, but he could take his time framing perfect shots.

The midday sun beat down. Sweat beaded on his forehead and dampened his hat. He'd be drenched by the time he finished today.

The village was in the Kalahari Desert, seemingly left behind by time. Only wildlife in search of food or adventure and tourists on safari visited.

He could imagine Jayne here with him.

With her appreciation of small things she would like this place and these people. She could appreciate the scenery surrounding them, the smells of the food boiling in the courtyard and the sounds of the music—a mix of vocals and stringed instruments. She would also love the animals. Maybe not the Puff Adder which had slithered across his path yesterday, but the mesmerizing zebras and playful meerkats would be right up her alley. She would also have gotten a kick out of the toilet at the luxury camp he'd first stayed in. It had been an actual throne.

Yes, he could picture Jayne enjoying herself here.

But she never wanted to see him again.

The day before he'd left for Africa he'd received her plane ticket in the mail, with a note saying she'd found her own way back to San Diego.

His chest tightened.

He refocused the camera on a group of children dancing barefoot on the dirt. The joy on their faces pulled at his aching heart.

He snapped more pictures.

A young boy stumbled. Hit the ground. Wailed.

A woman with a baby strapped to her back with colorful fabric rose from the group of adults and ran to the sobbing child. She brushed the dirt from the child's knees, wiped the tears from his eyes and kissed him.

He snapped a picture.

Love.

That was what he'd felt as he watched. That was the verb he'd captured.

It made him think of Jayne again.

Damn. He missed her. Each day he seemed to miss her more, not less.

He would be glad to get home. Not to San Diego, he realized, but to wherever Jayne was.

She was home now.

If only she would be waiting to welcome him…

That night in Vegas he'd told her she deserved more than he could give her. He still believed she deserved the best life had to offer and a better man to share it with her.

But the one thing she wanted, needed most, he knew he could provide.

Love.

It was as simple, as complicated, as that.

He loved her.

Tristan wasn't the man she wanted—he would never be the perfect husband of her dreams—but he loved her. He could be a husband who loved her completely.

But he'd never told her how he felt. He'd never given her the chance to decide for herself if love was enough. If he was enough.

I'm tired of you telling me what I want and what I need. I can take care of myself.

Jayne deserved a choice.

Tristan would give her that choice.

He only hoped he could live with her decision.

A big red "SOLD" was plastered over the real estate agent's "For Sale" sign on the lawn. Jayne's heart tripped with pride and excitement. After a week of offers and counter-offers, the cottage was hers. Well, almost hers.

The home inspector had found nothing to make her want to pull her offer. The agent had locked the house and left to contact the sellers.

As soon as the house closed escrow Jayne would own a home in San Diego.

One dream come true she could check off the list.

The corners of her mouth curved upward. She sat on the rickety porch steps, studying her new property.

The amount of work facing her was daunting, but Jayne couldn't wait to get started.

She surveyed the shaggy garden beds and straggling lawn. Weeding was a must, but everything else, including painting and repairing the white picket fence, could wait until the interior was completed. No sense moving items in only to have to move them out to remodel and refinish and paint.

She closed her eyes, imagining what the house would look like after all her hard work. The only thing missing was someone to share it all with.

You don't have to look. Someone will find you.

Jayne bit back a sigh.

"You look right at home."

Tristan. Her eyelids flew open. Her heart slammed against her chest. The air rushed from her lungs. Every single one of her nerve-endings stood at attention.

He stood outside the front gate, his hands shoved in the pockets of his wrinkled navy pants, the sleeves of his rumpled gray shirt pushed up onto his forearms. Stubble covered his face. His hair looked as if it hadn't been brushed in a couple of days.

He looked tired, tanned, great.

Jayne stood.

She wanted to fling herself from the porch steps and into his arms. But there was too much said and unsaid between them. Nothing had changed.

But, oh, was she glad to see him.

She ignored the pounding of her heart and smiled instead.

"I am home." She was about to tell him what the home inspector had told her, but decided not to. This was her dream, not his. "Well, it'll be my house as soon as escrow closes."

His steady gaze locked immediately with hers. "You bought the house?"

She nodded. Would he be glad for her? Or did her decision only underscore the differences between them?

His wide smile reached all the way to his eyes. He opened the gate and stepped inside. "Mrs. Whitcomb told me you were looking at a house today. I guessed it was this one, but I had no idea you were buying it. Congratulations. That's fantastic news."

That explained how he had found her.

But what was he doing here?

"Thanks. I would have never taken the plunge without your encouragement. You made me realize I can make my own dreams come true." Most of them. Not the hot, sweaty ones that plagued her at night, but the rest. Jayne stared at the "SOLD" sign. "And I am."

"I'm really happy for you."

He sounded sincere. His eyes were warm. She swallowed and looked away, down. "When did you get back from... Africa, was it?"

He nodded. "My plane landed about an hour ago."

Her heart thumped as she took in his wrinkled shirt, that movie star stubble. "You came straight here?"

"After a quick stop by your place."

"Where are your things?"

"In the car."

So he hadn't even checked into a new hotel yet. Her heart did a slow roll in her chest.

He took a step forward. "I didn't want to wait to see you."

"Why?" she whispered.

"You deserve everything you've ever wanted." He strode up the walkway until he stood in front of her. "You deserve a better man than me. You can probably find him, too. But I'm the one who loves you. I love you, Jayne."

He loved her.

She'd never expected to hear those words from his lips, but now that he'd said them she couldn't imagine not hearing them again. Joy flowed through her.

"You accused me of telling you what you wanted, what you needed, when we were in Las Vegas," he continued.

The beating of her heart was all she could hear. She wondered if he could hear it, too.

"But I'm offering you my heart, Jayne." He reached for her arm and took hold of her hand. "It's up to you to decide if that's enough."

He was giving her the choice.

Her spirits soared. Tingles burst through her like fireworks. He loved her. He really loved her.

It was all up to her.

Jayne's heart sang.

"Things don't make a family or a home. I have friends who are my family. A home can be anywhere there is love." She stared at the love shining in his eyes, love for her. She entwined her fingers with his. "Your heart is all I need, Tristan. Your heart. Your love."

He let go of her hand and embraced her. "Are you sure this is what you want?"

Jayne thought about her mom and the dreams they'd shared. She thought about what she'd gone through with Rich. She thought about her trip to Vegas with Tristan and the weeks without him since.

She completely trusted her judgment. She completely trusted her heart. She completely trusted Tristan. "I'm positive."

Her heart would be safe in his hands.

Tristan knelt on one knee. He pulled out a black velvet ring box, opened it, and removed a sparkling diamond solitaire. "I love you, Jayne Cavendish. I want to spend the rest of my life with you. Will you marry me?"

Happiness bubbled over. Love had found her. Her one true love. "Yes, I'll marry you."

He slipped the ring onto her finger. A perfect fit. "A good thing you said yes. I bought the ring in Africa. It would have been hard to return."

Jayne laughed. "I'm so happy I said yes, then."

He laughed, too.

"It's beautiful. Thank you." She stared at the breathtaking ring. The large diamond must have cost him a fortune. "Somehow I think you'll be contributing more to our finances, but I like knowing I'm bringing something to the marriage."

His tender gaze was practically a caress. He kissed her hand. "All I need is you."

"You don't mind, do you?"

"Mind what?"

"That I'm buying the cottage?" she said. "Maybe you'd rather live someplace else. Like the beach."

He kissed her hand again. "Anyplace where you are is home to me."

A sense of peace and contentment filled her. "I'll always be here waiting for you to come home."

"And when you come with me the house will be here, waiting for both of us to come home."

A bluebird landed on the gate of the picket fence. A breeze carried the scent of freshly mown grass from the yard next door. Children rode their bikes along the sidewalk, ringing their bells. Rays from the sun cast dancing prisms of light from her diamond ring on the house and yard.

They were home.

She smiled. "Yes, it will."

He swung her around, placed her on her feet and hugged her again.

In his arms she found a sense of belonging and home. She kissed him hard on the lips.

"If being engaged gets me kisses like that," he said, "I can't wait to see what marriage brings."

"I don't want to wait too long to get married," she said. "I know this is right."

"Then we'll have a short engagement."

She kissed him again.

"An even shorter engagement." He brushed the hair from her eyes. "Do you want to have a big wedding here in San Diego?"

She shook her head. Her dreams had changed. She didn't need the trappings of an expensive wedding. Not when she had the security of Tristan's love. "Not unless that's what you want."

"You're all I want."

She grinned. "No more neutral territory?"

"No separate bedrooms, either."

"I know the perfect place we should get married."

The glint in his eyes matched the glow in hers.

"Las Vegas," the two of them said at the same time.

EPILOGUE

STRAINS from the organist's version of Beethoven's "Ode to Joy" filled the wedding chapel at McKendrick's. The hunter green and gold décor provided a luxurious setting for the romantic ceremony. Sunlight streamed through the stained glass windows, as Jayne and Tristan made their way, arms linked, down the aisle after their wedding ceremony.

Tingles flowed all the way to the tips of Jayne's fingers and toes. She clutched the handle of her bouquet, a mix of white and pale pink roses.

The hem of her ballroom-length gown brushed the tops of her feet. The white silk and lace dress was simple, yet elegant, perfect for the afternoon's exchange of wedding vows.

Her friends' wide smiles echoed the joy in Jayne's own heart.

In the foyer outside the chapel Tristan twirled her into his arms. "Mr. and Mrs. Tristan MacGregor. I like the sound of that."

She leaned against him, feeling the beat of his heart. The rhythm matched hers. Opposites, yes, but love made up for all their differences. Love made up for everything. "Me, too."

"Good, because you're going to have to hear it for the next fifty years or so."

"Why don't we shoot for sixty?" she suggested.

"I'm game."

The wedding guests filed out of the chapel as the music spilled out behind them. The reception was being held upstairs on the roof at Sparkle. Alex had taken charge, carefully consulting Jayne and Tristan's preferences and working with the hotel's wedding planner to make sure everything would be perfect.

Knowing Alex, it would be.

"I'm so happy for you." Molly hugged Jayne, then looked at Tristan with a big grin. "I can't wait until we're back in San Diego."

"We're looking forward to it, too," he said, hugging her.

Jayne nodded. "I'm just so glad you're here. I know it can't be easy with a new baby."

"I would have come to see you married straight from my hospital bed," Molly said.

Baby Marcus, named for Linc's late brother, squealed. Molly took the two-week-old from her husband's hands. "He's hungry."

"That's one thing I'm not equipped to handle." Linc hugged Jayne and shook Tristan's hand. "Congrats. Once we're moved into the new house in San Diego we'll have you over for dinner."

"Once we finish remodeling we can do the same thing," Jayne said.

"Sounds great." Linc hurried to catch up to his wife and son.

Tristan leaned in toward Jayne. "Do you know how many people you have invited to dinner?"

She beamed. "Of course I do."

"We'll have to buy a bigger table."

"I was thinking the same thing."

Serena, who had been her matron of honor, practically exploded out of the chapel. The hem of her pink dress swirled about her legs. She looked more like a dancer than the first lady of Las Vegas.

"For the record." Serena's eyes twinkled as brightly as Jayne's engagement ring. "I told Jonas the two of you were meant to be together."

Jonas nodded. "She did."

Jayne hugged her exuberant friend. "Thanks, Serena."

"Thank you for proving me right." Serena hugged Tristan. "Jayne's a special woman. I trust you'll take good care of her."

"Promise," Tristan said.

Jonas shook his hand. "She's going to hold you to that promise."

"I expect her to."

Rich came through the chapel doors, walking with his remembered swagger. But his eyes, when they met Tristan's, were steady and clear.

"Guess you really *are* the best man, dude." He put out his hand. "Congratulations."

The two men embraced in a hard, double-pat hug.

"Thanks for coming, bud," Tristan said.

Jayne heard the emotion in his voice, and her heart swelled.

"I wouldn't have missed this for anything," Rich said sincerely. "Jayne." His gaze met hers. "May I kiss the bride?"

Smiling, she offered her cheek.

He brushed his lips lightly over her cheek and moved on, making a beeline for one of the more attractive wedding guests.

Jayne nudged Tristan and laughed.

Tristan squeezed her hand. "Thank you."

Her ex-fiancé was Tristan's oldest and closest friend. She was the one who had suggested they invite him. "He needed to be here."

"You're the best wife in the world."

She grinned. "That's all it takes?"

He laughed. "It's a good start."

Alex walked out of the chapel arm and arm with Wyatt. "Congrats," she said. "It was a lovely ceremony."

Jayne hugged her friend.

"Thanks for everything," Tristan said, before Jayne got the chance. "There's no place else we'd rather have had this wedding."

Alex beamed. "Wait until we get up to Sparkle."

"You don't want to spoil the surprise," Wyatt cautioned.

"Don't worry. Nothing could spoil today." Jayne stared up at Tristan. "It's a dream come true for me."

He smiled at her. "It's a dream come true for both of us."

HARLEQUIN Romance.

Coming Next Month

Available October 12, 2010

LARGER-PRINT BOOKS!

GET 2 FREE LARGER-PRINT NOVELS PLUS
2 FREE GIFTS!

HARLEQUIN® *Romance*®

From the Heart, For the Heart

HRLP10R2

HARLEQUIN®

A *Romance*

FOR EVERY MOOD™

Spotlight on

Inspirational

Wholesome romances
that touch the heart and soul.

See the next page
to enjoy a sneak peek from
the Love Inspired® inspirational series.

Autumn Granger gave her horse rein to slide toward the town's new sheriff.

"Hey, there." The man in a brand-new Stetson, black T-shirt, jeans and riding boots held up a hand in greeting. He stepped away from his four-wheel drive with "Sheriff" in black on the doors and waded through the grasses. "I'm new around here."

"I'm Autumn Granger."

"Nice to meet you, Miss Granger. I'm Ford Sherman, from Chicago." He knuckled back his hat, revealing the most handsome face she'd ever seen. Big blue eyes contrasted with his sun-tanned complexion.

"I'm guessing you haven't seen much open land. Out here, you've got to keep an eye on cows or they're going to tear your vehicle apart."

"What?" He whipped around. Sure enough, mammoth black-and-white creatures had started to gnaw on his four-wheel drive. They clustered like a mob, mouths and tongues and teeth bent on destruction. One cow tried to pry the wiper off the windshield, another chewed on the side mirror. Several leaned through the open window, licking the seats.

"Move along, little dogie." He didn't know the first thing about cattle.

The entire herd swiveled their heads to study him curiously. Not a single hoof shifted. The animals soon returned to chewing, licking, digging through his possessions.

Autumn laughed, a warm and wonderful sound. "Thanks,

I needed that." She then pulled a bag from behind her saddle and waved it at the cows. "Look what I have, guys. Cookies."

Cows swung in her direction, and dozens of liquid brown eyes brightened with cookie hopes. As she circled the car, the cattle bounded after her. The earth shook with the force of their powerful hooves.

"Next time, you're on your own, city boy." She tipped her hat. The cowgirl stayed on his mind, the sweetest thing he had ever seen.

Will Ford be able to stick it out in the country
to find out more about Autumn?
Find out in HIS HOLIDAY BRIDE
by bestselling author Jillian Hart,
available in October 2010
only from Love Inspired®.

FROM #1 *NEW YORK TIMES*
AND *USA TODAY* BESTSELLING AUTHOR

DEBBIE MACOMBER

Mrs. Miracle on 34th Street...

This Christmas, Emily Merkle (just call her Mrs. Miracle)
is working in the toy department at Finley's, the last
family-owned department store in Manhattan.

Her boss (who happens to be the owner's son) has placed
an order for a large number of high-priced robots, which
he hopes will give the business a much-needed boost. In
fact, Jake Finley's counting on it.

Holly Larson is counting on that robot, too. She's been
looking after her eight-year-old nephew, Gabe, ever since
her widowed brother was deployed overseas. Holly plans
to buy Gabe a robot—which she can't afford—because
she's determined to make Christmas special.

But this Christmas will be different—thanks to Mrs.
Miracle. Next to bringing children joy, her favorite activity
is giving romance a nudge. Fortunately, Jake and Holly
are receptive to her "hints." And thanks to Mrs. Miracle,
Christmas takes on new meaning for Jake. For all of them!

Call Me Mrs. Miracle

Available wherever books are sold
September 28!

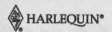

HARLEQUIN *Romance*®

BARBARA HANNAY

A Miracle for His Secret Son

Freya and Gus shared a perfect summer, until
Gus left town for a future that couldn't include
Freya.... Now eleven years on, Freya has a life-
changing revelation for Gus: they have a son,
Nick, who needs a new kidney—a gift only his
father can provide. Gus is stunned by the news,
but vows to help Nick. And despite everything,
Gus realizes that he still loves Freya.

**Can they forge a future together and
give Nick another miracle...a family?**

Available October 2010

www.eHarlequin.com

HRI7688